Goblin

All that glitters is not gold.

by Eric David Wallace

Follow the Adventure: **goblinfilm.com**

© 2025 Eric David Wallace

All rights reserved

CONTENTS

Gold Mine

It was a dark and stormy night. The mine was alive with the clatter of pickaxes and the murmurs of tired men. Shadows stretched long across the walls, flickering in the dim lantern glow. Dust hung in the air, thick as fog. Young Barry pressed forward, deeper into the tunnel. His bare chest was streaked with soot, and a flare atop his helmet burned like a small red star, lighting his path.

Then—something deep in the mine surrounded by darkness caught his eye. A glimmer in the rock, thin as a thread but unmistakably gold. He stepped closer, looked around making sure no one saw him draw close to it, he ran his fingers over the surface. A sharp pain shot through his fingertip. He pulled back, watching a single drop of blood swell, dark against the gold.

Barry glanced over his shoulder. The other miners hadn't noticed. He tightened his grip on his pickaxe and struck the stone with vigor. The first call sounded—the shift was nearly over.

He chipped faster. The gold spread beneath his blows, revealing something long and buried deep. Not ore. Not a nugget. Something else. The second call rang through the tunnels. The other miners were already making their way out.

Barry hesitated only a moment, then swung his pick with all his might. The rock split apart, and the object tumbled free, landing heavily in the dirt. Breathless, Barry knelt and reached for it. A sword—long, gleaming, its hilt still wrapped in timeworn leather. Strange symbols ran along the blade, their meaning lost to him, but the craftsmanship was unmistakable. This was no ordinary weapon.

He swallowed hard and wrapped it quickly in a burgundy cloth. The foreman's voice rang out, calling the last stragglers. Barry tucked the sword against his side and hurried toward the exit. Behind him, the tunnel shifted. Loose stones fell, revealing something carved deep into the rock—a single word, untouched by time.

GOBLIN

The Road to Nowhere

The morning sun cast long shadows across the driveway of a grand white estate, its golden features gleaming in the light, as Cash Harper heaved the last of Lin's Louis Vuitton luggage into the back of the VW bus. The old van groaned under the weight, its chipped blue paint flaking off onto the driveway. Lin stood nearby, watching with disgust; snapping her gum with sharp impatience. She ran a nail file over her already perfect manicure, scowling as Cash loaded his guitar case alongside the bags. 'I can't believe you lost your job, Cash!' she snapped. 'What am I supposed to tell my parents? That I'm dating a musician?'

Cash sighed, shutting the hatch with a firm thud. "Look, my friend booked us a nice cabin. Let's just try to have a good time." Lin rolled her eyes and marched toward the passenger door. "Great! Unemployed and going on vacation." Nearby, Dan wiped his hands on an old rag and closed the engine compartment. His thick glasses slipped down his nose as he gave Cash an enthusiastic thumbs-up. "Okay! Everything looks good. We're ready to roll!"

He clapped Cash on the shoulder with a reassuring grin. "Don't worry, man. You'll find a new job in no time. Besides, you've been wanting to play more music, right? Now you've got plenty of time!" Cash forced a smile and nodded. He wasn't sure if Dan's optimism made things better or worse. Dan's girlfriend, Ivy, had already jumped into the backseat, her short black hair tousled by the breeze. She grabbed Dan's hand and pulled him in after her, giggling as they tumbled into the cushions.

Lin, perched stiffly in the front seat, set down her nail file and turned to glance at them. Her expression flickered—just for a moment—with annoyance and jealousy. She said nothing, just turned back around and crossed her arms. It was Lin's voice, sharp and impatient, that first broke the warm hum of the journey. "You've been dating for over five years, and you're still acting like children!"

Cash, the smile never leaving his face, hopped into the driver's seat. His eyes twinkled with the spark of someone about to set out on an adventure. "Everybody ready?" he asked, his voice as cheerful as the morning sun. "We're ready!" Dan and Ivy shouted together, their spirits high and voices full of excitement. But Lin, ever the skeptic, just shook her head. "Not really," she muttered, settling back into her seat with an air of quiet resistance.

Cash gave her a quick grin, his enthusiasm undeterred. "We're all going to have a great time, right, guys? Let's do this!" With a turn of the key, the VW bus came to life, its engine rumbling like a sleepy beast waking from its slumber. Cash eased the vehicle out of the driveway, the tires crunching softly against the gravel, and soon they were gliding down the road.

The highway stretched endlessly ahead of them, a ribbon of dust and asphalt unwinding into the horizon. The sun hung high, a golden orb in a blue sky, casting long shadows on the earth below. Cash looked over his shoulder. "Check out my new song, *Cream Puff*. Who knows, it might be a hit some day." He cranked the music up, a lively tune that made the bus hum with energy. Dan and Ivy, unshakable in their joy, began to sing, their voices filling the space with the carefree abandon of youth. But Lin, with arms crossed tightly, sat silent, her gaze fixed on the passing scenery, as if searching for something hidden just beyond reach.

As the road wound through the hills, Cash's eyes caught sight of a great pothole in the distance, but it was too late. The bus jolted violently, sending Lin's head crashing against the ceiling with a sharp "Ouch!" The sound of something breaking followed, a piece of the taillight snapping off and skittering across the asphalt like an omen. "Oh! Sorry, didn't see that coming," Cash called over his shoulder, his voice tinged with regret.

Lin glared at him, but her words were drowned out by the rush of wind as Cash, Dan, and Ivy rolled down their windows, arms and faces eager to meet the breeze. Ivy, with her head thrown back, smiled widely, her hair dancing freely in the wind like golden strands of sunlight. Dan, eyes wide with wonder, turned to Cash. "I can't believe Cheveyo got us a cabin at the last minute," he said, incredulous. "I tried to book one myself, but everything was taken."Cash shrugged with a knowing smile. "He's been living up here for a while now. He's got connections in places you wouldn't believe."

The mountains rose around them, vast and mysterious, cloaked in vibrant orange wildflowers that seemed to stretch forever. Above them, a red-tailed hawk soared through the brilliant blue sky, its wings cutting through the air with effortless grace, following their little bus as it wound its way along the winding road.

At the gas station, Cash stopped to fill the tank, his hands moving quickly and efficiently, as if he had done this a hundred times before. Dan and Ivy wandered into the store, leaving Lin alone in the backseat. She was busy brushing her hair, searching for any stray strands, her eyes distant and unfocused.

She cracked the window slightly, the cool air rushing in, but then quickly slammed it shut with a shudder. "Ew, gross! Yuck!" she exclaimed, disgusted by the sudden intrusion of a bug. Her eyes flicked nervously to the flyers pinned on the telephone poles outside. Each one bore the face of a missing child, their expressions frozen in time, and Lin couldn't shake the unsettling feeling that seemed to settle in the air.

Cash paused as he topped off the tank, his gaze lingering on one of the flyers. The name and face seemed to hold his attention for a moment longer than necessary. Then the sharp blast of Lin's horn broke his reverie. "Can we go already?" Lin called, her voice edged with irritation. "The bugs are trying to eat me!"

Cash sighed, his hand twisting the gas cap back into place before he climbed into the driver's seat. The engine hummed to life, and he pulled the bus away from the pump, glancing briefly at the old man sitting on the bench near the entrance. The man watched them with unblinking eyes, his pipe smoke curling lazily into the air, and for a moment, Cash couldn't shake the feeling that he was being watched by someone who knew more than they let on.

Inside the bus, the mood lightened. Dan and Ivy passed over an assortment of snacks, but Lin only accepted the water, her face softening slightly as she took a sip. "Just the water... thanks," she said quietly, though her tone still carried a hint of sharpness. Cash settled into his seat, his excitement palpable. "Okay, buckle up, everyone," he said, his eyes twinkling. "We should be there in twenty minutes."

Dan and Ivy, oblivious to Lin's mood, dove into their treats, their laughter and chatter filling the space. "Oh, yeah, this is soooo good!" Dan exclaimed, crumbs flying from his mouth. "I love vacation!" Ivy turned to Cash, offering him some of her corn nuts. "Want some?" "Yes, please!" Cash said with a grin, stretching his arm back towards her. She poured a generous pile into his hand, and as he pulled the bus back onto the road, he tossed a few into his mouth, savoring the salty crunch.

As the bus rumbled forward, a gust of wind caught the corner of one of the missing child posters, and it fluttered free, spinning into the air like a ghost in the wind. Cash glanced back at it briefly before his eyes returned to the winding road ahead, the sense of something forgotten—something important—settling heavy in the pit of his stomach.

The Cabin

The wind whispered through the towering trees that surrounded the modest cabin, their branches swaying like ancient sentinels keeping watch over this quiet corner of the world. Beneath the shade, the forest moved with secrets—shadows and rustling leaves, where small creatures darted through the underbrush, vanishing into the heart of the woods.

The blue VW bus screeched to a halt, its tires crunching against the gravel with an almost eager sound. Cash leapt out of the driver's seat, his black boots landing firmly on the loose stones beneath him. The others followed, pouring out from the bus with a rush of energy, each one eager to stretch their legs after the winding journey.

"Look at this place!" Cash exclaimed, throwing his arms wide, as though embracing the beauty of the view. "Isn't it incredible, Lin?" Lin raised her cell phone as if the device could capture the whole sweeping landscape in one frame. She spun in a slow circle, her eyes scanning the horizon. "What? No reception?!" she cried, panic edging her voice.

She darted here and there, each step becoming more frantic as she searched for a signal. The wind tousled her hair, and the trees seemed to mock her, standing silent and still while the rest of the group laughed, easing into the carefree atmosphere of the weekend. Ivy and Dan were already unloading snacks from the bus, their laughter mixing with the rustling of the leaves.

"This is going to be a long weekend..." Ivy muttered with a grin, casting a glance at Lin's flustered movements. Dan, unbothered by the lack of reception, pulled out a cigarette, lighting it with his Zippo. He took a slow drag, the smoke curling in the air like a lazy river.

"Yes... it certainly will be," Dan said, his voice thick with amusement. Lin, having found a flicker of signal, brightened immediately. "Yes! Look, I've gained more followers!" she shouted with delight, holding her phone triumphantly aloft. Her joy was short-lived. As she bounced on her toes, eager to show the world her accomplishment, she tripped over a thick tree root. Her arms flailed wildly before she tumbled backward, the phone slipping from her grasp as her excitement turned to dismay.

"No, no, no!" she cried, scrambling to regain her balance. "I lost it!" The roar of a Ford Bronco arrived like an unexpected thunderclap, kicking up a cloud of dust that swirled in the air, momentarily enveloping Lin in a hazy fog. She coughed and waved her hands in front of her face, her frustration growing as the dust settled.

Out of the Bronco stepped Cheveyo, a man in his early thirties, his long hair flowing like a dark river down his back. He wore a silver necklace that gleamed faintly in the afternoon sun. His smile was broad, friendly, as if this was a long-awaited reunion. "Cash, my friend!" Cheveyo called out, his voice carrying a warmth that echoed in the open air. Cash's face lit up as he strode over to him, arms opening wide for a hearty hug. "It's been too long. Thank you for making this happen," Cash said, clapping him on the back.

Together, they walked toward the bus to grab the luggage, their voices mingling with the rustling of leaves as the others followed.

"This place is amazing!" Dan said, his eyes scanning the surroundings in awe. "How did you find it?" Cheveyo grinned, his eyes twinkling with the mystery of the mountains. "Well, it wasn't easy. The landlord... well, he's an odd one, you know. But hey, you must be Lin," he added, extending his hand to the woman who was still fumbling with her phone.

Lin barely looked up, still absorbed in her world of digital connections. "Hi," she muttered, offering a half-hearted handshake. "I've heard a lot about you," Cheveyo continued, his voice carrying the sound of a secret untold. "It's good to meet you in person." Lin studied him for a moment, her gaze lingering as though trying to unravel his presence. She offered a small smile, though it didn't reach her eyes. "Nice to meet you too," she said, her tone polite but distant. "I like your style. Who's your stylist?"

Cheveyo laughed, the sound rich and genuine. "The Salvation Army," he replied with a wink, clearly amused by her curiosity. Lin blinked, caught off guard by his unexpected response. She said nothing but nodded in acknowledgment. Cheveyo motioned for them to follow. "This way, everyone. The cabin's just over here. Let's get our things settled, and then we can go for a hike before the sun sets."

As they made their way toward the cabin, Lin struggled with her heavy luggage, the wheels barely making it up the porch steps. Cash, ever the gentleman, stepped forward to help her. "Let me," he said, taking the handle of her expensive suitcase with ease. Lin let out a relieved breath as Cash set the suitcase inside. He returned to the bus, lifting Lin's Louis Vuitton luggage from the roof rack. The weight of it nearly bent him in half, the bag heavy as if filled with the weight of expectations. With a grunt, he managed to lower it to the ground, and a cloud of dust exploded from the impact.

"Need help with that?" Cheveyo called from the porch, concern lining his voice. Cash waved him off, though the strain was visible in his posture. "Ah, it's my back. I had a motorcycle accident last year... slipped discs in my neck now," he explained, though he spoke with a matter-of-fact tone, as if it was an old injury no longer worth dwelling on. Cheveyo stepped forward, his hands steady as he took the heavier bag. "I've got this," he said. "You take the smaller one."

Lin didn't seem to notice their efforts, still engrossed in her search for a signal, her phone in her hands like a lifeline to a world that felt increasingly distant. Inside the cabin, the scent of pine and wood greeted them—a rustic charm with all the modern amenities hidden beneath its weathered walls. Lin, with a decisive air, made her way to the master bedroom, her eyes scanning the room for any sign of comfort. Her gaze flicked to the guest bedroom, and the bunk beds there, before she turned on her heel and hurried back to claim the larger room.

"Guess I'll take the master," she said, tossing her Chanel purse onto the bed, claiming the space as her own. Cash, caught off guard by her sudden decision, hesitated. He exchanged a look with his friends, but Dan merely shrugged, offering a sympathetic grin. "Don't worry about it," Dan said, his voice a quiet murmur to Cash "Ivy and I can take the bunk beds." Cash nodded gratefully, the tension easing from his shoulders as he grabbed Lin's luggage and slowly carried it into the master bedroom. Ivy whispered to Dan, her voice light but filled with concern, "I don't know how he puts up with her..."

Cash placed Lin's Louis Vuitton luggage on the floor with a heavy thud, the sound echoing in the small cabin room. Lin didn't seem to notice, her attention fixed firmly on her phone as she stood by the window, her eyes scanning the distant mountains beyond. Her thumb moved quickly across the screen, trying in vain to reconnect with the digital world that seemed so far out of reach.

"I thought they said it was supposed to be a nice cabin," she muttered under her breath, her voice barely audible over the quiet rustle of the forest outside. Cash smiled, a bittersweet expression that hinted at his familiarity with the way she always seemed to want more—never quite satisfied. He didn't say anything, though. He simply reached out, gently tugging on her arm, guiding her back toward the bed.

Lin stumbled slightly, her surprise evident as Cash took a step backward and fell onto the bed, pulling her down with him in the process. "Aah!" Lin yelped, her voice sharp and unamused. "Don't do that! I'm mad at you! No job, no five-star hotel, and no signal!" She sat up quickly, her arms crossing over her chest in a clear sign of defiance.

Cash chuckled softly, brushing a strand of hair away from her face with a tender touch. "When was the last time you did something adventurous, Lin?" he asked, his voice light but full of genuine curiosity. She raised an eyebrow, a look of contemplation crossing her features as she took in his question. For a moment, it seemed as though she was trying to find the right answer, something that could push back against his gentle teasing. Finally, she sighed.

"Well, I once got lost on a cruise ship when I was ten," she replied with a hint of a smirk. "My parents were pissed! But they finally found me in the jewelry shop. "Cash laughed at the image of her as a ten-year-old causing such a commotion, the sound of his laughter bright and carefree, a stark contrast to Lin's usually stiff demeanor.

Lin stood, smoothing her clothes and glancing at herself in the mirror. Her eyes flickered over the bracelets, rings, and necklaces she wore, each piece a testament to her sense of luxury. The cabin's rustic charm seemed lost on her—just another backdrop to her world of high-end living. "Cheveyo's calling us," Cash said after a moment, his tone warm, but laced with a trace of resignation. Lin sighed dramatically, rolling her eyes. "Of course he is."

But, despite her complaints, she followed him without protest, stepping into the living area of the cabin where the others were already gathering near Cheveyo. Outside, the group had already formed a loose circle around Cheveyo, who stood with a wide grin on his face. His hands were outstretched, as if he were presenting something extraordinary. The crisp mountain air filled the space, and the surrounding forest seemed to hold its breath, waiting for whatever revelation was to come next. "Ladies and gentlemen," Cheveyo said, his voice carrying an undertone of mystery that immediately grabbed the group's attention. "This way. You're in for a beautiful surprise." He turned on his heel and started down a narrow path that wound through the forest, his steps confident, his movements sure. Dan raised an eyebrow, a skeptical look on his face. "You're not going to get us lost, are you?" Cheveyo laughed, the sound rich and low, like distant thunder. "Nope! I've been here a hundred times." Dan and Ivy exchanged a glance, but they followed without hesitation, hand in hand. Cash reached for Lin's hand, his fingers gently wrapping around hers. She sighed again, but didn't pull away. It was clear that the adventure ahead held little interest for her, but she walked beside him nonetheless, her mind elsewhere.

The forest around them grew denser as they walked, the tall trees rising like ancient giants, their branches reaching upward toward the sky. The air was thick with the scent of pine, and the ground beneath their feet was soft, damp from the morning dew. The group moved forward in silence, the only sounds the distant calls of birds and the soft crunch of leaves beneath their shoes. Cheveyo led them into a small clearing where the sunlight filtered through the canopy above, casting dappled shadows on the forest floor. "Look at all the pine trees," Cheveyo remarked, his voice filled with quiet reverence. "This place is a paradise for squirrels." Dan and Ivy turned their attention to the trees, watching as a squirrel darted across a fallen log, its tail flicking nervously before it disappeared into the higher branches. Dan reached out toward a nearby flower, eager to touch its delicate petals, but Cheveyo's voice quickly stopped him.

"Oh, no," Cheveyo warned, raising a hand. "Don't touch that one. The Corn Lilly is extremely poisonous." Dan quickly pulled his hand back, a sheepish grin spreading across his face. "Good to know." Cheveyo smiled, unfazed by the interruption. "Let's keep moving. The lake's just ahead." Lin rubbed her forehead in irritation, a clear sign of her impatience. "How much farther?" she asked, the edge of frustration in her voice. Cheveyo smiled, unaffected by her tone. "Just through those bushes." They continued forward, passing through a tunnel of thick branches and leaves that seemed to stretch endlessly. The forest closed in around them like the walls of an old cathedral, the shadows growing deeper as they moved. Finally, as if the forest itself had granted them access, the trees parted, revealing a breathtaking view.

Before them lay a sparkling lake, its surface gleaming like liquid silver in the fading light of the day. The group stood in stunned silence, taking in the beauty of this hidden paradise. It was a place untouched by time, a serene sanctuary where the world seemed to stand still, waiting for its secrets to be uncovered. Lin, her phone still gripped tightly in her hand, paused in the clearing. For a brief moment, her eyes widened, and her mouth hung slightly open as she took in the scene before her. There was a flicker of something in her gaze—perhaps awe, perhaps a fleeting sense of wonder. But it was gone almost as quickly as it had come, swallowed once more by the digital world she could not escape.

The Lake

The group emerged from the dense forest, one by one, stepping out into the open with awe on their faces. The lake before them gleamed like a silver mirror under the sun's warm glow, stretching far beyond the horizon. "Whoa! You weren't kidding. This is beautiful!" Cash exclaimed, his voice full of wonder as he took in the breathtaking view. Lin, however, was already absorbed in her phone, framing the perfect shot. "This is going to look so awesome on my profile!" she murmured to herself, snapping several pictures as she posed with exaggerated flair.

Dan and Ivy, too, joined the chorus of digital record-keepers, their phones capturing the moment, though they seemed more present than Lin, who was lost to the whims of the digital world. Cash walked over to Cheveyo, who had seated himself on a large rock, gazing serenely across the lake. His eyes were soft, as if taking in not just the view, but something deeper within it. "I never knew this lake existed," Cash remarked, his tone filled with genuine surprise. Cheveyo nodded, still staring at the water. "It's a hidden gem. That's why I wanted this cabin. You can't get to it from the other side—it's a bit of a secret spot."

Cash nodded, looking around. "It's gorgeous." Cheveyo glanced toward Lin, who was now swatting at the bugs surrounding her. He raised an eyebrow and subtly nodded in her direction. "So," Cheveyo said with a small grin, "you think she can make it through the weekend?" Cash turned his gaze toward Lin, who was struggling to take selfies while keeping the pesky bugs at bay. His face softened with a quiet understanding. "Ah, well, she lives a pretty sheltered life," Cash muttered, not wanting to speak too harshly.

Cheveyo chuckled, a deep sound that reverberated from within. "I can see that... How's she taking your job situation?" Cash's expression tightened, the weight of his recent loss settling in his chest. "Not so good." Cheveyo nodded sympathetically, the silence stretching between them before he spoke again. "What happened with your job, anyway?" Cash sighed, his fingers absently tossing a smooth stone in his hand. "Well, I was a senior designer at that big toy company for ten years. Then they brought in some new management. They told me I was overpaid, overqualified, and they laid me off... Just like that."

Cheveyo blinked in disbelief. "Just like that?" Cash nodded, tossing the stone across the surface of the lake. It skipped, making several small leaps before sinking into the water with a soft plop. "Bummer," Cheveyo remarked. "Yup," Cash agreed quietly, watching the ripples on the water. Cheveyo, ever the optimist, handed Cash another perfectly smooth stone, one that seemed made for skipping. "Sometimes... you need to be faced with a situation like this to have a better view of where you really want to go, and what you really want." Cash looked at the stone in his hand, turning it over as though it might reveal some hidden truth. It was smooth, perfectly flat, an odd kind of beauty to it.

"I know I can get another job... I just don't want to rush into it. I've always had this dream of being a musician. Ever since I was a kid. Back in high school, I had this little three-piece band. We won first place at the talent show. It was cool, but... Lin would never accept it if I really went for a career in music."

Cheveyo looked at him thoughtfully, his gaze turning inward for a moment. "My grandpa used to say, 'You can only dance around your destiny for so long before fate pulls you in.'" Cash's eyes turned distant, focusing on the lake's farthest point as he reflected on the words. He turned the stone in his hand again, contemplating its weight. "I've got another quote that's been stuck in my head for the last ten years," Cash said softly, almost to himself. Cheveyo looked over, curious. "What's that?"

Cash's gaze softened further, a fleeting smile crossing his lips. He stared out at the glittering surface of the lake, the setting sun casting a golden glow across the water. "All our dreams can come true, if we have the courage to pursue them." He threw the stone with all his might, watching as it skipped effortlessly across the water, its flight so graceful that it seemed to stretch the boundaries of time. They watched in silence until the stone finally vanished from view.

Cheveyo looked on, amazed. "Who said that?" Cash turned to Cheveyo, a mischievous glint in his eye. "Walt Disney." Dan approached the pair, his attention caught by something on the other side of the lake. "See that up there?" he said, pointing toward the top of a mountain. "What's that?" Cheveyo shielded his eyes from the sun, squinting up at the peak. "That's Gold Mountain," he said, his voice carrying a hint of something mysterious. "There's a bunch of old mines up there. They say that the whole place is cursed."

Lin, overhearing, rushed over to where Cheveyo and Dan stood, her curiosity piqued. "Did you say gold? Do you think we could still find some?" Cheveyo chuckled darkly, shaking his head. "I doubt it. And if the rumors are true, trust me—you don't want to go up there." Lin's eyes narrowed. "What rumors?" Cheveyo leaned in slightly, as though sharing a secret. "Legend says a Goblin used to live up there. He'd steal children, take people's gold, and hide it deep in the mines." There was a beat of silence as the group absorbed his words. Lin burst out laughing, her skepticism evident. "A Goblin? That's ridiculous!" Cheveyo stood and gestured toward the trail, a knowing smile on his face. "Let's head back. It's getting late."

Cash's eyes lingered on the mountain for a moment longer, a strange glimmer of light reflecting off something near the mine, something that didn't quite belong. Before he could take another good look, Lin grabbed his hand, pulling him away. "C'mon, I'm tired. And I'm hungry," she said with a huff, her irritation apparent. Cash glanced at her, but followed, the moment of curiosity fading as he gave in to Lin's urgency. As the group made their way back through the forest, the sky turned to shades of pink and purple, the light dimming in the distance. Ivy, walking alongside Lin, showed her some of the pictures they'd taken by the lake. "Hey, Lin, check out these photos," Ivy offered, her voice light and cheerful.

Cash moved ahead to join Cheveyo, and as they walked, the two of them continued their conversation. "I never knew there were stories about Goblins in Big Bear," Cash mused, still intrigued by the strange tale. Cheveyo chuckled softly, his voice taking on a more casual tone. "There's a lot of strange things around here. Goblins, UFO sightings, cults… you name it." Cash's curiosity deepened. "But you're not worried?" Cheveyo's grin widened. "Nah. Don't worry about any of that stuff. This weekend's about forgetting our problems. Some old friends of ours are coming over tonight, and I've got some new magic tricks to show off. It's going to be a great time."

Cash smiled, the excitement of the weekend creeping back into his chest. "Oh yeah? Still doing magic, huh? I always loved magic. I've got a few new tricks of my own!" Cheveyo's grin became even wider. "Alright then, tonight we'll celebrate with a magic show!" As they reached the cabin, the last of the sun's rays dipped below the horizon, casting a soft glow across the path ahead. As the evening sky began to deepen, the warmth of the cabin seemed to contrast the chill of the night creeping in. Inside, the smell of spices and sizzling meat filled the air as Dan and Ivy busied themselves in the kitchen, preparing skewers for the night's meal. Cash stood in the doorway, watching for a moment before he spoke.

"Do you guys need any help with that?" he asked, his voice cutting through the quiet hum of activity. Dan glanced over his shoulder, a smirk on his face. "No, thanks, we're good. Go out there and check on Cheveyo." Cash nodded, the weight of the day's adventures still settling on his shoulders. He grabbed two root beers from the fridge, the cold bottles comforting against his palms. As he stepped outside, the air felt crisp against his skin, the moonlight casting shadows that danced with the rustling trees.

Cheveyo was crouched by the fire pit, adjusting the stones with a careful hand. He moved with practiced ease, a man in tune with the rhythms of nature. When Cash approached, he handed him one of the root beers. "Here you go, Cheveyo," Cash said, offering the bottle. Cheveyo paused for a moment, giving Cash a soft smile. "Oh, no thanks, I don't drink too much these days." Cash shrugged, unconcerned. "Neither do I, it's just a root beer." In a moment of agreement, Cheveyo accepted the bottle, his eyes twinkling with humor. "Well, in that case, here's to good times. Cheers!" The two clinked their bottles together in a quiet toast to the night ahead. The fire crackled in the distance, the flames casting a warm glow across their faces.

Cash leaned back slightly, his gaze sweeping over the serene landscape. "Thank you for booking the cabin. It's beautiful out here. It's really nice to get away to a place like this." Cheveyo's smile widened, a glint of nostalgia in his eyes. "No problem! That's what friends are for, right?" He chuckled softly. "I'll never forget that time I broke up with Molly and you gave me that birthday card with you posing in the buff... like this..." He turned his back to Cash, raised his finger to his lips, and struck a playful pose. Cash burst out laughing, his face lighting up at the memory. "Yeah, I knew I had to do something to cheer you up." Their laughter echoed in the cool air, an easy camaraderie between old friends. Cheveyo poured some gasoline on the firewood, lighting the match with a practiced flick of his wrist. The flames leaped to life, casting shadows that flickered across their faces.

Cash's eyes wandered across the yard, catching sight of the RV trailer in the distance. A soft light shone through its windows, and squinting, Cash saw the silhouette of a man moving inside. The figure paused, pouring himself a drink, before disappearing from view. Before Cash could think too much on it, the sound of footsteps broke his concentration. A group of friends appeared around the corner of the cabin, carrying camping chairs and coolers of beer. Cash stood up, his face lighting up at the sight of them.

"Hey, guys, long time no see!" he called out, his voice carrying a warm welcome. Erik, a skateboarder with long hair and a mischievous grin, approached first. The two shared a secret handshake, a gesture of friendship that had survived the test of time. "Yeah, man, it's been awhile. How you been?" Erik asked, clapping Cash on the back. "Hanging by a thread," Cash replied, a wry smile tugging at his lips. Erik laughed heartily. "Haha! Yeah, man, I know what you mean." The rest of the group joined them, and there were more hugs and smiles exchanged. They popped open their beers with a chorus of cheers, the clink of bottles a happy sound beneath the crackling of the fire. "Cheers!" the crowd toasted together, the warm glow of the fire reflecting in their eyes, their voices rising in celebration. Inside the cabin, Lin turned the shower on, the steady hum of water filling the small bathroom. She carefully removed her gold ring, placing it on the bathroom counter. As she undressed, the ring's reflection caught the light, slowly fogging up in the steam. Her image was blurred for a moment, fading into the mist as she stepped into the shower, disappearing behind the curtain of water.

The Campfire

Cheveyo stood tall, his back to the fire, his arms stretched wide as if summoning the very night itself. The flames danced in his eyes, casting long shadows on his face. "Come closer, everyone!" he called out, his voice carrying over the crackle of the fire. The group shuffled closer, their faces glowing in the firelight. Cheveyo raised his drink, a small but dramatic gesture.

"A toast," he said, his voice ringing with the joy of the moment. "To Cash! To new beginnings, and to the mysteries we've yet to uncover!" Without warning, Cheveyo blew a cloud of gold dust into the flames. The fire flickered and snapped, flaring up for a moment like something alive. The group laughed and cheered, their spirits lifted by the magic of the night. "Now," Cheveyo continued, his smile fading into something more serious. "Every campfire deserves a story, doesn't it?"

The group leaned in, their faces eager with curiosity. Cheveyo's eyes twinkled as he surveyed them. "A good story," he said, lowering his voice, "Isn't just for entertainment. It's for warning... for the unknown that lurks beyond the edge of the firelight." A hush fell over the group. Even the wind seemed to hold its breath. "I'll tell you a tale," Cheveyo said, his voice dropping to a whisper, "Of the creatures in the woods, who watch and wait. Some of them are friendly, some are not. But there's one that no one ever wants to meet. The Goblin." A sharp silence followed his words. Ivy raised her hand, her voice full of both wonder and worry.

"Cheveyo," she asked, "What exactly is a Goblin?" Cheveyo's smile was small but knowing. He looked into the fire, as if seeking the right words. "A Goblin," he began, "Is not like anything you've ever seen. It's a creature born of the earth, old and hungry. They live in the dark corners of the world, drawn to treasure—gold, jewels, anything that glitters." The flames crackled louder, as though to underline his words. "They have eyes that see in the dark, and feet that move like shadows. They can be quick as the wind, and as sly as a fox. And if they ever want something from you, you best hope you never offend them."

A nervous chuckle bubbled up from the group, but Cheveyo's gaze remained serious. "If you do," he went on, "They'll curse you. And the curse is not something you can shake off. Not so easily." Ivy's eyes widened. "A curse?" she asked, her voice barely a whisper. "Yes," Cheveyo said, his voice heavy with the weight of the words. "A curse that binds you, makes you see things that aren't there, things that drive you mad." The group fell silent, the air thick with the mystery of Cheveyo's words. "But there is one way to break the curse," Cheveyo added. "One way to stop the Goblin. You must catch it and dip it in holy water." "Holy water?" Dan asked, his voice skeptical but intrigued.

Cheveyo nodded, the firelight flickering in his eyes. "Yes. But there's more. You can only do it on the holiest of nights—when the moon is full, and when the air is thick with magic." The group murmured among themselves, their eyes scanning the dark sky above them, where the full moon hung like a ghostly lantern. "You can't kill a Goblin," Cheveyo said, lowering his voice to a near whisper. "Not like any other creature. You must trap it, bind it, and hope it's merciful. If not…" He let the words trail off, unfinished. Erik, always ready for a joke, jumped to his feet and struck a playful pose. "What if I challenge it to a skateboard contest?" The group laughed, the tension breaking, but Cheveyo held up his hand. "No matter how you fight it," he said, "The Goblin will always be stronger than you think. Never forget that."

As the laughter faded, Cheveyo smiled again, his expression softer now. "But tonight, my friends, we leave the Goblins behind. Let's enjoy the night and the magic in the air. Cash, please take the stage." The group cheered, their spirits lifted once more, but Cash remained silent, his gaze lost in the flames. Then, stepping in front of the fire, he spoke. "I need a volunteer," he said, his voice carrying the same weight that Cheveyo's had just moments before. The group turned to him, curious. Cash looked around, his gaze landing on Ivy. "You," he said, his voice almost a whisper, "Will you join me?" Ivy stood slowly, a mix of excitement and nervousness in her expression. She walked toward Cash, her heart pounding in her chest. Cash smiled. "Do you have any cash?" he asked, his tone playful.

Ivy laughed nervously, patting her pockets. "I do, actually." She pulled out a crumpled one dollar bill and handed it to him. Cash took it, then turned to the fire. He held the bill in one hand and waved the other over it, muttering something low and strange. The fire flickered brighter for a moment, and to everyone's astonishment, the bill rose into the air, spinning slowly. The group gasped in awe as the bill floated before them, then gently fell back into Cash's hands. "Behold," he said, "From one to ten." He unfolded the bill, and there it was: a ten-dollar bill instead of the one Ivy had handed him. Ivy's eyes went wide as she took the bill, her mouth hanging open in surprise. "Magic," she breathed, staring at it in disbelief.

The group cheered, their laughter ringing out through the night, but Cheveyo raised a hand again, calling for quiet. "It's late," he said, his voice soft but firm. "Tomorrow brings its own mysteries. It's time to rest." The group groaned, but they slowly began gathering their things, heading back to their cabins as the fire sputtered and died. Cash lingered by the fire, staring into the dying embers. His thoughts were far away, lost in the shadows of the night, where secrets still waited to be uncovered.

Goblin

The smoke from the campfire curled upwards, a feeble glow fading into the night. A small shadow crept across the forest floor, moving stealthily toward the cabin. It stopped. Then, a tiny head poked up into the moonlight, revealing two pointed ears. A rabbit. In a flash, the rabbit sprang into the underbrush, disappearing with a soft rustle. The shadow stirred, paused, and then, with careful steps, crept past the dying embers of the fire, its movement barely a whisper. It glided up the steps of the porch, a silent figure in the moonlit night.

It stopped at the bowl of milk, its clawed finger dipping into the cool liquid. It tasted. "Mmmmmmhh..." The voice was a soft rasp, a strange hum of pleasure. The shadow picked up the bowl, tipping it to its lips. A loud slurp echoed through the stillness. Suddenly, the creature choked, sputtering as a piece of red gum shot from its mouth, flying through the air in a sharp arc before landing with a wet plop on the ground. The creature coughed, a sound that seemed to shatter the calm of the night. "Akkkkk!!" The goblin's eyes narrowed in frustration.

In a swift motion, it hurled the bowl into the air, sending it crashing to the porch floor where it shattered into pieces. The back door of the cabin creaked open, letting in a sliver of moonlight that spilled across the kitchen floor. The shadows of the room seemed to shiver, trembling with the presence of something unseen. The goblin's shadow crept across the tiles, its small form flickering in the glow. The fridge door swung wide, and in a flurry, jars, cans, and vegetables flew from their places, colliding with the countertops. Ketchup sprayed onto the oven, milk splashed across the floor, the room a chaotic mess in a matter of moments. The goblin's laughter, a low and guttural sound, echoed through the destruction, and as it made its way toward the door, it kicked over a garden gnome with a careless sneer. "Hahahah!" The goblin's laugh hung in the air, dark and unsettling.

Outside, the crickets' chirps returned to the night, though they were quieter now. The clock on the wall ticked slowly, its hands frozen at "3:33." Morning light poured into the cabin, spilling over Dan as he stepped off the bunk bed, rubbing his eyes. Still half asleep, he wandered toward the front door, drawn by the fresh air. He opened the door, breathing in deeply, a smile forming on his face as he took in the view.

Cash appeared from behind him, pausing as his gaze fell on the mess in the kitchen. He blinked, then raised his foot, seeing a lettuce leaf stuck to his toe. "What in the world...?" Cash muttered under his breath. Dan, lost in the beauty of the mountains, didn't notice the wreckage behind him. "I know..." Dan's voice held a dreamy quality. "That's why they call it 'The Great Outdoors.'" "Not over there!" Cash gestured at the kitchen with a wave of his hand. "I mean in here!" Dan turned, his eyes widening when he saw the mess. "What's that?" he asked. Cash pointed at the lettuce on his toe. "The mess," Cash added, his voice tinged with disbelief. Dan's eyes followed the motion, and his jaw dropped. "What... the devil happened in here?"

Ivy, hearing the commotion, stepped out of the bedroom. Dan motioned toward the kitchen, his eyes still on the chaos. "This is... not good." Cheveyo appeared next, rubbing his eyes as he came toward the kitchen. He looked over the scene, his brow furrowing as he spotted the gnome, now tipped over and lying in an awkward position. "This is no animal's doing..." Cheveyo's voice was low, a hint of caution in his words. He approached the gnome, gingerly picking it up by the legs and inspecting it closely. He set it down, facing everyone. On its forehead, a tiny, peculiar footprint was embedded in the clay.

Everyone leaned in, their faces filled with confusion. "What kind of footprint is that?" Ivy asked, eyes narrowing. Cheveyo stood, turning his gaze toward the rest of the kitchen. "This wasn't an animal. It was something else." Dan glanced over at Ivy, unsure of what to make of it all. "What's going on here?" he asked, his voice tinged with worry. Ivy stepped forward. "Something—or someone—broke in."

Cheveyo, still kneeling by the gnome, raised an eyebrow. "But nothing's been stolen…" Lin stepped into the room, wearing flashy white pajamas, her gold bracelets catching the light. She eyed the disarray, her eyes widening. "Oh, no. We have to call the police!" She pulled her phone from her pocket and began dialing, but Cash stepped in. "Remember, no reception here," Cash reminded her. "And nothing's missing."

Lin frowned, holding up her finger, which was missing a ring. She waved it in the air. "What about this ring? It was right here yesterday." Dan and Cash exchanged glances, a ripple of concern passing between them. They began to gather up the mess in silence, though their minds were elsewhere. Cheveyo, noticing a broken piece of the bowl outside, stepped outside to investigate. As Cheveyo returned, holding the piece of the bowl, he turned it over in his hands, inspecting it carefully. "Look at this…"

Lin's eyes shot up from her phone. She recognized the piece of gum on the bowl. Her stomach twisted. Cheveyo raised an eyebrow. "Red gum. That's strange." Cash crossed his arms, casting a side glance at Lin. "The only one who chews gum around here is… Lin." Everyone turned to her. She avoided their gaze, still staring intently at her phone. "Well, what was I supposed to do?" Lin's voice wavered defensively. "It was dark! I thought it was an ashtray. Besides, that's nothing compared to the mess in here. My ring is still missing."

Cheveyo shook his head, disbelief etched on his face. Cash stepped forward, his expression grim. "Clearly, whoever did this wanted to mess with us. We should talk to the landlord. This might not be the first time something like this has happened." Lin huffed, her frustration mounting. "I want to talk to the landlord now!" she demanded. Without waiting for a reply, she stormed toward the front door. The others, still processing the events, stayed behind. Lin turned, glancing back at them. "Come on! We need to get to the bottom of this, Cash!" Cash, calm as ever, gestured toward the door. "Relax. Just calm down for a minute. Follow me, and I'll take you to the landlord's trailer."

Barry the LandLord

The sun was just beginning to rise, casting a soft, golden light over the rolling hills. Cash stood at the door of the old RV, his hand raised to knock. Behind him, his friends gathered—Dan, Ivy, Cheveyo, and Lin—each looking around with wide eyes, taking in the quiet, rustic setting. It was the kind of place you'd expect to find in a story, the kind of place that made you feel like you were on the edge of some great adventure. Cash knocked on the door with a cheerful tap. A moment later, it creaked open, revealing Barry, the landlord. He was an older man, with a face lined by age and a robe of indigo blue draped over his thin frame. His feet were snug in white tabi socks, and his eyes blinked at them with something between curiosity and annoyance. "Yeah, what do you want?" Barry grumbled, his voice raspy, as if the very air of the trailer had dried it out.

Cash smiled warmly. "Good morning, sir. We're renting the cabin next door. These are my friends—Dan, Ivy, Cheveyo, and Lin." He gestured to each of them, and they waved in return, though Barry barely lifted a hand. "Hi…" Barry muttered in a tone that suggested he'd rather be anywhere but here. "This morning when we woke up," Cash continued, trying to sound as casual as possible, "the kitchen was a complete mess. Someone must've broken in and trashed the place last night. We were wondering if you might have seen or heard anything."

Barry squinted at them, clearly trying to piece together what was happening. "Has this ever happened before?" Cash pressed. Barry scratched his chin, pausing for a long moment as if deep in thought. But before he could speak, Lin stepped forward, hands on her hips, her voice dramatic. "Someone stole my ring! There's a criminal on the loose! You need to do something about it!" she exclaimed, though the sparkle of her many rings seemed to suggest she wasn't in any immediate danger.

Barry's gaze dropped to the shiny jewelry around Lin's wrists and neck, then shifted to the broken milk bowl lying on the porch. His eyes flicked back to the group, and for the first time, a flash of concern passed over his face. "Oh… I'm sorry about that," he said with a weary sigh. "I'll go have a look. Sometimes raccoons or other animals wander in. But you kids go on and enjoy the day—I'll take care of everything." Cheveyo let out a sigh of relief, grinning. "Thanks, Barry! You're a lifesaver." Cash nodded, smiling as well. "Much appreciated, sir."

Without another word, Barry disappeared behind the door, securing it with a soft click. Cash turned to Cheveyo, a wide grin spreading across his face. "That wasn't so bad," Cash said, his voice light. "He doesn't seem so bad after all. I think that went well." Cheveyo gave a playful shrug, his eyes glinting with mischief. "Yeah, let's go get changed, and then I'll take you all to the meadow. Who's ready for an adventure?" Lin scowled, rolling her eyes. "Great. A raccoon stole my ring. Perfect." Barry shuffled around the cramped RV, muttering to himself. His slippers scraped against the wooden floor as he passed by an old bookshelf. It was filled with strange objects and dust-covered books from places far and wide. He moved the shelf with a grunt, revealing a secret compartment behind it. From a hook in the wall, he took a large, rusted keyring, choosing the one silver key from the pile of old, worn-out ones.

He slipped the key into a hidden lock behind a picture on the wall. With a click, the wall parted, revealing a narrow stairwell leading down into shadows. Muttering under his breath, Barry descended the stairs, his footsteps echoing in the silence. The room was filled with dust and cobwebs, a forgotten space holding strange relics from distant lands. Barry pushed past boxes and old trunks, grumbling the entire time. "Those kids have no idea what they've gotten themselves into," he muttered, tossing boxes over his shoulder.

At last, he spotted what he was looking for: a rusted chest, ancient and heavy. With a grunt, he dragged it out, opening it with a squeal of protest. Inside, wrapped in a faded cloth, was an object that seemed to pulse with a strange energy. He scowled at it. "This cursed thing," he said, his voice thick with disdain. "I can't even look at you…" With a grunt of effort, he wrapped the object carefully in the cloth and made his way back upstairs. Barry emerged from the hidden room, the mysterious object pressed tightly against his chest. He peered out the window, watching Cheveyo and the others disappear into the woods, laughing as they went. He hesitated for just a moment before stepping outside, making his way to the cabin.

The sun was bright and cheerful, casting a warm glow over the little cabin. Barry moved quietly around the porch, his boots crunching on the dirt as he knelt by the campfire. Small footprints marked the ground, leading off into the trees. Barry ran his fingers over the dirt, his mind working furiously. "Hmmm…" he murmured. With a swift motion, he unwrapped the cloth, revealing a gleaming golden sword. It was unlike any weapon you'd find at a local market—its surface was worn and weathered, yet it still radiated a faint, otherworldly glow.

Barry smiled to himself. "I knew it," he muttered under his breath. "I knew it." He stood, his gaze shifting toward the flower bed. It had been torn apart, petals scattered like confetti. He walked toward the front door, squinting at the shattered milk bowl on the porch. Barry stepped inside, his boots making soft thuds as he crossed the threshold. The kitchen was in complete chaos—food and debris strewn across the floor, the air thick with the smell of spilled milk. His eyes landed on a piece of the broken milk bowl, with a red gum stuck to it. He picked it up, sniffed it, and grimaced as the gum stuck to his fingers. "This isn't good," Barry muttered to himself. "Not good at all. Looks like someone's been stirring up trouble."

A Moon in the Meadow

The group had finally reached the top of the hill, where a wide expanse of tall yellow flowers stretched across the meadow below. Their vibrant hues swayed gently in the breeze, the peacefulness of the place settling over the group like a blanket. The quiet hum of nature filled the air, until a sudden notification bell from Lin's phone broke the stillness. She reached for her purse in excitement. "Oh, my gosh, I got reception!" Lin exclaimed, pulling out her phone and lighting up with an influx of messages. The others remained absorbed in the stunning landscape.

Cash smiled, gazing at the meadow. "This is beautiful. There's so much to discover here," he said, his voice soft but filled with wonder. Cheveyo, who had been silent for a moment, pointed toward the distant trees. "Let's go this way. There's supposed to be an old abandoned church over there." Cash glanced at Lin, still glued to her phone. With a small shrug, he turned to Dan and Ivy. "You guys want to come?" Dan, already kneeling to photograph the flowers, shook his head. "Look at all these flowers. We'll hang with Lin and take some photos here until you guys get back." Cheveyo waved dismissively. "We'll be back soon. It's not far."

Cash turned back to Lin, who flicked her hand toward him without looking up. "Go ahead," she muttered, her gaze never leaving the screen. With a final glance at Lin, Cash nodded, and he and Cheveyo made their way down the hill. They passed through the sea of yellow flowers, the air thick with the scent of pollen, butterflies fluttering in the breeze. The beauty of the place felt magical, and Cash felt alive, as though every step he took was in tune with the earth. "Let's go up that hill over there for a better view," Cheveyo suggested, pointing toward a rise in the distance. "Okay, I'll race you!" Cash said, already eager for the challenge. Cheveyo chuckled. "You still think you can beat me?" Cash smirked. "One way to find out."

Without another word, he sprinted ahead, the wind in his hair, heart pounding in his chest. He didn't look back, but the sound of Cheveyo's footsteps grew distant behind him. Cash pushed himself harder, his legs burning, but as he neared the crest, he felt a tug on his sleeve—Cheveyo had caught up. The two of them stumbled to a stop, panting heavily. Cash, with a triumphant grin, jumped to his feet, raising his arms to the sky. "Wahoo! I'm the king of the hill!" Cheveyo groaned, bent over with his hands on his knees. "Just like old times, huh? I knew you couldn't beat me."

They both laughed, their voices echoing across the hill. Cheveyo stood up and wiped his brow, scanning the landscape. "Hey, look over here," he said, crouching near a patch of flowers. Cash, however, was transfixed by a yellow butterfly that fluttered past him, its wings catching the light. He followed it as it flew toward an opening in the trees. "Hey, wait up!" Cheveyo called from behind. Cash didn't answer. He couldn't pull his eyes away from the butterfly. There was something mesmerizing about it—something familiar. Without thinking, he followed it down the path, the trees growing denser and the air cooler as he ventured deeper into the woods. The smell of earth and moss filled his lungs. It was quiet here, in a way that felt different from the meadow—an underlying tension in the air.

Then, as if by magic, he saw her. A woman, barely visible through the trees. She was dressed in a colorful dress, her dark hair flowing in the wind like a river. Cash froze, his breath caught in his throat. She was beautiful in a way that seemed almost unreal. The world seemed to hold its breath, and for a moment, nothing else existed but her. She turned toward him, their eyes meeting. Her gaze was calm, almost knowing, as if she had been waiting for him. She raised a hand in a silent invitation.

Without thinking, Cash stepped toward her. His heart raced, and his mind screamed for him to stop, but something in her presence held him there, rooted to the spot. "Follow me," she said, her voice soft but clear, gesturing down the path. Cash felt an overwhelming sense of calm, a feeling that told him to trust her without question. He stepped forward, following her as she moved with fluid, almost ethereal grace. But when he looked up, she was gone.

The trees stood silent. The world around him seemed to shift. A chill ran down his spine. Had she been real? He scanned the area but saw nothing. "Cash! Where are you?" Cheveyo's voice broke through the disorienting silence. Cash turned, suddenly disoriented. "I'm here!" Cheveyo appeared at the edge of the trees, concern etched on his face. "What's going on? You okay?" Cash blinked, shaking his head. The forest seemed to close in on him, the colors of the trees and the sky swirling. But he couldn't speak of the strange encounter—not yet. He simply nodded, forcing a smile. "I'm fine. Let's head back."

They turned and began walking back up the path, Cash glancing over his shoulder one last time, half-expecting to see the woman. But she was gone. When they reached the edge of the trees, the warmth of the sun brushed against Cash's face. He squinted into the light—and there she was again. A woman stood just beyond the trees—dressed in flowing colors that rippled in the breeze. Her long, dark hair seemed to move in slow, graceful waves, as if caught in an unseen current. She didn't speak. She only moved lightly through the brush, her hands grazing the petals of wildflowers. Cash glanced back. Cheveyo was nowhere in sight. When he turned forward again, the woman was watching him, her presence feeling otherworldly. Her gaze held him. She raised a hand in greeting. He hesitated, then waved back.

She pointed toward the hilltop. Cash followed her gaze. Perched atop the hill was an old well, weathered with time, a small white cross resting on its stones. Without a word, she started up the hill, Cash didn't think—he simply followed. At the summit, they stood before the well. Cash leaned over the edge, peering into the darkness. He picked up a small rock, letting it slip through his fingers, listening for the splash below. A faint echo reverberated from the depths. There were words carved into the well's surface, buried beneath dead leaves. Cash brushed them aside. The inscription read:

True light lies within.
Constructed January 3, 1801.

"The water here is holy," the woman said. Cash turned to her. "Holy water?" She nodded. "It's not here by chance. These lands hold a history few know." "Can you drink it?" "Yes… if you can reach it." Cash ran his fingers over the inscription, his mind racing with questions. There was something in the way she spoke, like she was telling him more than she let on. "There's a lot of superstition surrounding this well," she added. "What kind?" Cash asked. She met his gaze, her eyes searching him. For a moment, he felt exposed—like she could see through him. "I feel an energy in you," she murmured. "But something is holding you down. You seem… stuck."

Before Cash could respond, Cheveyo's voice called out. "Cash! Where are you?" Cash turned toward the voice. "I'm here!" Cheveyo appeared, eyes narrowing with concern. "What's going on? Is everything okay?" "What's your name?" Cash asked, still looking at the spot where the woman had stood."Moon," she answered. Cash turned to her, intrigued. "Where are you from?"

She opened her mouth to answer, but before she could, Cheveyo's voice rang out again. "Cash! I'm over here!" Cash turned back to the woman, but she was already walking down the hill, moving with quiet, effortless steps. She glanced over her shoulder once before disappearing beyond the trees. Cheveyo reached his side. "Did you find something?" Cash exhaled deeply, glancing down the hill.

"Yeah… a beautiful girl." Cheveyo followed his gaze. "Where?" "She was just here. Over there. Now she's gone." Cash pointed down the hill. "She said her name was Moon."

Cheveyo raised an eyebrow. "Moon? Interesting…" "What?" "In Native culture, the Moon is the protector of the earth. Its spirit watches over us… sometimes changes our fate." Cash felt a shift within him at the words. He turned back to the well. "What's that?" Cheveyo asked. "A Holy Water well," Cash murmured. "Moon led me here." Cheveyo stepped closer. "This must be where the old church used to be. Guess this is all that's left." He checked his watch. "We should get going. Before your mystery girl turns to stone." Cash smirked, though doubt lingered. "You think she's not real?" "I think we've been out here too long." Cash took one last glance, hoping for another glimpse of Moon. But she was gone.

The Offer

The meadow was bathed in the soft warmth of the afternoon sun as Cash and Cheveyo returned, their footsteps crunching on the grass as they neared the others. The sight of Lin, deep in conversation with two strangers, caught Cash's attention. The couple—Mike and Linda—were in their mid-50s, both dressed in pristine white linen, exuding an air of quiet wealth. Linda, holding a delicate white parasol over her head, leaned in slightly as she spoke, her laugh light and almost musical. Mike, sporting a crisp white Panama hat, sipped from a crystal wine glass, the contents a shimmering pale hue.

Cash's eyes narrowed as they approached, sensing something strange in the air. "Cash, just in time!" Lin said, catching sight of them. She handed Cash a bottle of water, pulling him into the conversation with ease. "I'd like you to meet my new friends—Mike and Linda. They own a major toy company in New York." Cash hesitated for a brief moment, then extended his hand toward them. "Hello, nice to meet you," he said cautiously, trying to mask his discomfort. Mike grinned widely, shaking his hand firmly. "Cash, so nice to meet you!" he said, his voice booming with enthusiasm. Linda, her smile warm but somehow too eager, added, "Your girlfriend told us so much about you! Sounds like you're a very talented designer, working at such a prestigious company for all those years."

Cash, still unsure about these strangers, forced a polite smile. "Yeah, it was a fun job, but..." Before he could finish his thought, Lin interjected, clearly excited. "Well, Cash, Mike and Linda were just telling me they're looking to hire a new senior designer for their toy company. They pay very well!" "Is that right?" Cash asked, his tone skeptical as he took a slow drink from his water bottle, his eyes flicking between Lin and the couple. Linda smiled, her eyes twinkling. "We start our senior designers at a million dollars a year, plus bonuses," she announced casually, as if it was no more remarkable than ordering a cup of coffee.

Cash nearly choked on the water, sputtering as it splashed down the front of his shirt. Lin quickly grabbed a tissue from her purse, dabbing at his face with a mix of concern and amusement. She nudged him gently from behind with the purse, an almost silent command to play along. "Cash, why don't you get their contact information?" she said, her voice a little too bright. Linda reached into her bag, producing a clean white business card with an odd pink logo on it. She handed it to Cash with a smile. "Why don't you hang on to this, Cash? Give it some thought and let us know if you're interested." Cash stared down at the card in his hand, the logo for "EUPHORIA—Toys for Girls and Boys" printed in soft, swirling letters. He turned it over, seeing Linda's contact details, along with the company's website. The card felt strange in his palm, as if it didn't belong there. Mike and Linda, meanwhile, continued sipping from their wine glasses, oblivious to his discomfort.

Mike clapped Cash on the shoulder with a jovial chuckle. "Cash, I know a winner when I see one. The moment I saw you, I knew you've got what it takes. And that girlfriend of yours... uh-huh... very impressive." Cash stood frozen for a moment, still processing the whirlwind of the conversation. What was this all about? He couldn't quite grasp the gravity of the situation, and part of him felt like he was in a strange dream. Lin nudged him again with her purse, this time more insistently. "Say something, Cash!" she urged. "Oh, uh, thank you, thank you... very much," Cash stammered, still in disbelief. "I'll... take a look at your website and get back to you guys." Mike grinned, holding up his wine glass in a toast. "Oh, yeah, no rush, buddy. Remember... first class is the only way to fly through life." He gave Cash a knowing wink. "You guys enjoy the sunshine. We're looking forward to hearing from you, Cash."

Mike and Linda strolled off, their white linen catching the breeze as they sipped their wine, leaving Cash standing there with the business card still in his hand, feeling more bewildered than ever. Lin slapped him lightly on the arm, her voice urgent. "Cash, you've got to take this more seriously! Those people are top-level industry executives! And they just offered you the job of a lifetime!" Cash didn't respond. His gaze was distant, lost in thought as the reality of what had just happened settled uneasily in his chest. He looked around at his friends, but they were silent, watching him with the same uncertain curiosity. It was Cheveyo who broke the stillness, stepping forward with a calm demeanor. "Well, you got their business card, Cash," Cheveyo said, giving him a reassuring smile. "You've got plenty of time to think about it. Come on, guys, let's head back for lunch. I know a great place in town."

The group started walking back through the meadow toward the cabin. But as they moved, something caught Cash's attention. He glanced up to see a white dove soaring through the sky, its wings outstretched in perfect grace. It landed on a nearby branch, its soft cooing filling the air as it began to sing. Cash reached into his pocket and pulled out a guitar pick, turning it over in his fingers. The business card was still in his other hand, the two objects side by side.

He studied them for a moment, lost in thought. The bird's song continued, sweet and melodious, but then, with a sudden shift, it fell silent. Cash looked up to see the dove gone, its presence as fleeting as the moment. Inside the cabin, the atmosphere was quieter, a sharp contrast to the conversation outside. Barry, grumbling under his breath, was in the midst of cleaning, his movements quick and agitated. He checked under the bed, behind the curtains, and in the cupboards, his eyes darting nervously. "Damn thing," he muttered, "where are you hiding?" Finally, after a thorough search, he gave a frustrated sigh and locked the door behind him, a troubled look settling on his face as he glanced around one last time. Something was wrong, but he couldn't quite put his finger on it.

Sushi and Secrets

The blue VW bus rumbled up the dirt road, pulling to a stop outside an old restaurant that resembled a dilapidated cabin. The peeling wood and crooked sign spoke of years of neglect, but it was clear this was their destination. The group spilled out of the bus, with Cheveyo holding the front door open for them. Lin, lowering her oversized sunglasses, stepped inside first, scanning the place with an incredulous look. "You've got to be kidding me," Lin muttered under her breath as she walked in.

Inside, the restaurant was small but packed with customers. Old photographs of fishermen proudly displaying their catches lined the splintered walls, while a hodgepodge of taxidermied animals sat on display, their glassy eyes fixed in eternal stares. The smell of fried food mixed with the musk of dust, creating an oddly familiar, if not unappealing, atmosphere. A waitress bustled over, carrying drinks for everyone. Dan, parched, took a large gulp of his soda. He paused for a moment, then let out an enormous belch, so loud and prolonged that it caused the entire room to fall silent. The eyes of every customer turned toward him.

Lin's face contorted with disgust as her jaw dropped. Her gum slipped from her mouth and plopped into her water glass. The rest of the group burst into laughter, but Lin remained silent, staring daggers at Dan. A large, burly man with a black beard and a round belly—Black Beard—rose from his seat and made his way toward the table. He grabbed Dan by the collar, lifting him clean out of his chair.

"I can tell you're not from around here. Time someone taught you some manners, boy," Black Beard growled.

Black Beard raised his fist, ready to strike. But before anything could happen, Cash, reacting instinctively, kicked a chair across the floor. It slammed into Black Beard, causing him to stumble backward and crash to the floor with a loud thud. The entire room went still, and Black Beard's cronies shot to their feet, ready for a fight. Cash's friends stiffened, fear rising in their chests. Just then, the door swung open, and Barry, the landlord, strode into the restaurant with an imposing presence. The wind blew in behind him, sending napkins swirling through the air. The locals froze at the sight of him, their faces filled with a mix of fear and respect. Whispers spread like wildfire. "Black Beard, I can see your life hasn't changed much. Still scumming around on the floor. Didn't I tell you to never come in here again?" Barry's voice rang out across the room.

For reasons unknown to Cash, Black Beard and his friends suddenly seemed terrified of Barry. The large man scrambled to his feet, avoiding Barry's gaze. "Uh... Oh... Sorry," Black Beard muttered. "Go on! Get outta here!" Barry barked. Black Beard, flanked by his crew, scrambled out the front door, desperate to put as much distance as possible between himself and Barry. The tension in the room faded, but Cash and his friends were left in stunned silence, watching as the intimidating figure of Barry moved toward their table. "OK if I join you?" Barry asked, his voice casual but authoritative. "Yes, of course!" Cash quickly pulled up a chair for Barry. "Thank you for saving us. Those guys were about to kill us," Cash said, his voice filled with genuine gratitude. "Don't worry about them. They're just a bunch of losers," Barry replied, waving a dismissive hand.

Pam, the waitress, came by to take Barry's order, a practiced smile on her face. "Hi, Pam. I'll have the usual," Barry said, as if everyone in the room knew what he meant. "You got it, Barry, coming right up! What about for the rest of you?" Pam asked, glancing at the group. "I'll take the special," Cheveyo said. "Burger for me," Cash added. "We'll have the special, too," Dan and Ivy said in unison. "Salad, no dressing, please," Lin said, her tone flat as she avoided looking at Barry. "All right, you got it, coming right up," Pam said, jotting down their orders before walking away. As Pam disappeared into the kitchen, Barry turned back to the group, his expression softening slightly. "Well, I finally cleaned up the place. Searched high and low, and there's nothing to be worried about. Found some raccoon tracks outside the cabin, though. Those pesky little critters get into everything," he said, sounding almost proud of the accomplishment.

He grabbed Lin's water and took a big gulp, but as he swallowed, he choked and spat out her red gum into a napkin. "What the devil is that?! Who's gum is this?" Barry exclaimed, holding up the napkin as if it were a foreign object. "Oh, it's mine. Sorry," Lin muttered, her face flushing with embarrassment. Barry glanced at her, disgust flickering across his face. His gaze dropped to the napkin, where the red gum lay like a foreign object. He realized, perhaps too late, that it was Lin's gum that had angered the Goblin. Lin, trying to avoid Barry's eyes, focused on her phone's mirror, carefully applying a layer of nude lipstick.

Pam returned with Barry's sushi rolls and the rest of the meals. She set everything down, smiling brightly. "Here you go, everyone. Enjoy!" Pam said cheerfully. "Thank you, Pam," Barry replied, his voice warm. Barry joined his hands in an exaggerated gesture, as though preparing for something ceremonial. "Itadakimasu!" he said, as though the meal was a sacred ritual. He ripped open his chopsticks and began to devour his sushi at an alarming pace, chewing with his mouth open and spilling crumbs everywhere. His guests tried their best to eat, but they found it difficult to focus with the spectacle before them.

Before anyone could say anything, Barry had finished his meal, wiped his mouth with a napkin, and stood up, ready to leave. "Well, I hope you guys enjoy your stay. I'm gonna go set out a couple of raccoon traps before it gets dark," Barry said, without missing a beat. With that, he left the table and walked out the door, leaving his guests to process the strange encounter. The group exchanged wary glances. Pam returned to clear Barry's plate, a knowing look on her face. "Don't worry about the bill. Barry put it on his tab. Can I get anything else for you guys?" she asked, already anticipating their needs. Everyone exchanged looks of surprise. "I'll take an iced tea?" Ivy asked, still a little taken aback by the events. "You got it," Pam said with a smile before walking away.

As Pam disappeared into the kitchen, Cash spoke up, his voice quieter now, almost to himself. "Well, that was strange, but I guess Barry's not so bad." "At least he paid for our meal," Dan added, trying to lighten the mood. "There's something odd about that guy," Cheveyo muttered, his eyes narrowing slightly. "I like him," Ivy said, shrugging. "He eats like a pig!" Lin shot back, her voice tinged with annoyance. Cash glanced around the table, his eyes flicking to each of his friends. "Well, one thing's for sure. The locals get nervous around him," he said, his voice thoughtful. The group sat back, silently processing the events that had just unfolded. It was clear

Barry was a man to be reckoned with, and Cash wasn't sure whether to be grateful or terrified.

The Boatride Begins

It was a bright, sunny afternoon, and the group stood on the wooden dock, their swimsuits glistening in the sunlight. Around them, the small fishing boat bobbed gently in the water, ready for adventure. Lin stood at the edge, her arms folded, clearly uncertain. She glanced at the boat, then back at her friends, her face scrunched with doubt. "I'm not getting on," Lin said firmly, shaking her head. "I don't like boats, Cash."

Cash smiled and held out his hand, trying to reassure her. "It's perfectly safe, Lin. We have life vests on board." Lin hesitated, but eventually, with a sigh, she took Cash's hand. The boat rocked as she stepped onto the edge, and in a split second, she teetered dangerously toward the water. Cash quickly grabbed her arm, steadying her. "Thanks," Lin mumbled, looking a little embarrassed. "Don't mention it," Cash said, grinning.

Behind them, Ivy and Dan tried their best to stifle their laughter. Cheveyo, standing at the helm, clapped his hands together. "Alright, everyone ready for some fun?" His voice was full of excitement. "Here we go!" With that, the boat pulled away from the dock, Cheveyo steering them slowly out into the lake. The water was calm, and the gentle rocking of the boat felt peaceful. "This is a nice boat, Cheveyo," Cash said, leaning back in his seat. "How'd you get it?"

Cheveyo grinned. "It's a friend of mine's. He's got a place up here, lets me take it out on weekends when he's not using it." "That's nice!" Cash said, admiring the boat. They cruised slowly through the no-wake zone, passing other boats, float tubes bobbing with fishermen, tourists in canoes, and families in aluminum boats. A few strange-looking mountain folk waved from a party boat. "So," Cheveyo called over the engine's hum, "what do you wanna do first? Fishing, or wakeboarding?" "I'm in for wakeboarding!" Dan shouted, practically jumping out of his seat. "Wakeboarding!" Ivy cheered, pumping her fist.

Cash nodded. "I'll give it a go, too." "Well, it looks like wakeboarding wins," Cheveyo said, smiling. "Lin, what about you?" "Fishing?" Lin suggested, though it was clear she didn't have much enthusiasm. Cheveyo shook his head. "Sorry, Lin. You're outnumbered. Who's first?" "I'll go!" Dan volunteered, practically leaping into the water. He gripped the rope, and Cheveyo revved the engine, pulling Dan forward. After a few clumsy splashes, Dan finally found his balance and glided smoothly across the water. Cheers erupted from the boat.

Next was Ivy, who, after a few wobbly attempts, managed to stay on her board long enough to ride the wake. More cheers followed. Cash was up next. With a confident grin, he grabbed the rope, and in one smooth motion, was up and soaring across the water. He even tossed in a small jump, just for fun. The others cheered loudly, though Lin only clapped half-heartedly, her eyes rolling as she looked away. "I bet I can do that," Lin muttered under her breath. "Alright, Lin, you're up," Cash said, grinning. "Go show us what you got!"

Lin took the rope, and as Cheveyo gunned the engine, the boat pulled her into the water. But on her very first try, she was flung off the board, face-planting into the water with a loud splash. When she surfaced, her eyes were filled with tears, and Cheveyo quickly circled the boat around to pick her up. "Are you okay, Lin?" Cash asked, concern in his voice. "Want to try the inner tube instead?" Lin shook her head, her lips quivering. "No." "Alright," Cheveyo said with a grin, "who wants to try the inner tube?" He glanced at Dan and Ivy. "We do!" they shouted in unison, grinning. "Let's do it!"

Cheveyo sped up the boat, and with a sharp turn, the inner tube flung Dan and Ivy into the air before dropping them back into the water with a splash. Their laughter filled the air, and Lin finally gave in, deciding to join the fun. As the boat circled again, Lin's expression softened, and she actually managed a small smile. "Anyone need a bathroom break?" Cheveyo asked, glancing back at the group. Dan, Ivy, and Lin raised their hands. "Yes, please!" they all chimed. Cheveyo guided the boat toward the sandy beach, where a public restroom waited. As they hopped out, Cash gazed up at the hills in the distance, his eyes widening as he noticed something sparkling in the sunlight. "Hey, is that the gold mine up there?" he asked, pointing toward the mountains. "It's closer than I thought."

Cheveyo followed his gaze. "Yeah, that's one of them. See that trail? It leads right up to the mine." Cash squinted. "It looks like it's all fenced off, though." Cheveyo nodded. "Yup. They don't want anyone up there. It's a restricted area." As Cheveyo opened the cooler to grab a bottle of water, he tossed it to Cash, who caught it easily. "Seems like Lin loosened up a little after that slam, huh?" Cheveyo grinned. Cash chuckled. "I hope so. The day's not over yet." Soon enough, Dan, Ivy, and Lin returned to the boat. Cash grinned at them. "Snack time, everybody!"

As they passed around snacks, Cash reached into his backpack and handed Lin a bag of veggie chips. "Here you go, Lin. I made sure to bring something healthier." Lin inspected the bag, made a face, and handed it back to him. "I don't like this brand. But thanks anyway." Cash's smile faded slightly, but Ivy perked up. "I'll take them! I love veggie chips!" Cash handed the bag over to Ivy, who happily munched on the chips. "Mmm… these are good!" she said, her voice full of approval. "Alright, everyone," Cheveyo said, steering the boat away from the shore, "time to fish before the sun sets. Let's head to the other side of the lake."

The group settled in, Lin lying back on the boat, wearing a straw hat and sunglasses, clearly exhausted. The sky above them shifted from purple to orange to magenta, reflecting on the still waters below. Cash was the first to feel a tug on his fishing pole. "Wahoo!" he exclaimed, reeling it in. When the fish broke the surface, it shimmered in the sunlight, a beautiful rainbow trout. "Are you really going to eat that thing?" Lin called out, not looking up from her relaxed position. "Yep," Cash said proudly. "Trout's great. It's healthy."

Cheveyo nodded. "You can barbecue it tonight. It'll taste amazing roasted over a fire." As the group continued fishing, Cash caught four more fish while the others had little luck. Holding up his stringer of fish, Cash grinned. "Well, this should be enough for everyone, right?" Cheveyo grinned back, admiring his friend's catch. "Definitely. Well done, my friend." Dan pulled out his camera. "Let me get a photo of you, Cash," he said. Cash posed on the edge of the boat, the mountains in the background, holding up his fish proudly. Dan snapped the photo just as Cash looked over at Lin. She was looking the other way, seemingly uninterested. After a moment, she turned around and gave a half-hearted clap, her smile forced and fake.

Cash's grin faded as he returned his gaze to the sunset, his heart sinking a little. But the lake shimmered with the setting sun, and the adventure wasn't over yet. Not by a long shot.

The Weight of the Flute

Lin yawned and reached for the lamp on the nightstand. Its soft light illuminated her face, casting a gentle glow. She straightened her hair in the mirror, the reflection of her tired eyes meeting her own gaze. Slowly, she undid the clasp of her shiny jewelry, placing it carefully on the nightstand beside a bottle of water. She took a sip of the water, the cool liquid refreshing her. The window was open, and the curtains fluttered lightly with the breeze. As she turned to retrieve her jewelry box from her luggage, she noticed something was wrong. The pieces of jewelry she'd just set down had disappeared. Her heart skipped a beat. Shocked, she spat the water from her mouth, spraying it across the mirror, and screamed. "Ahhhhhh!"

The door to the room opened abruptly. Cash stood in the doorway, startled by her scream. "What happened?" he asked, eyes wide with concern. "My jewelry!" Lin's voice was panicked. "My new diamond bracelet, my earrings, all my rings... they're gone! I put them right here!" She pointed frantically to the empty space on the nightstand. Cash looked at the spot she indicated, but there was nothing there. He started searching the room, his eyes scanning every corner. "Are you sure you didn't take them off on the boat?" he asked, trying to stay calm. "After what happened yesterday? No way!" Lin's tone was sharp. "My jewelry comes with me everywhere I go! This is all your fault, Cash. I didn't want to come here in the first place. This is turning into a nightmare."

Cash attempted to comfort her, but Lin was beyond consolation. Her frustration exploded, and she kicked the desk lamp, sending it flying across the room. "That's it! I'm done with this place, and I'm done with you!" With a shove, she pushed Cash out of the room, slamming the door behind her and locking it with a force that left him standing in stunned silence. "Ugh!" Lin muttered to herself as she paced the room, her eyes wild with disbelief.

Her gaze fell upon the curtain, which was partially pulled out the window, the fabric billowing in the breeze. A growing sense of suspicion washed over her. Slowly, she walked toward the window and peered out cautiously, scanning the surroundings, both left and right. The moon hung full and bright in the clear sky. Outside, a group of friends from the previous night were gathered around the fire, sharing food and drinks, their laughter drifting through the night air.

Cash stepped out of the cabin and immediately noticed the dozens of animal traps scattered across the property, some large, others small, each one set in a different way. "Geez, there are more traps out here than people," he muttered to himself. He carefully maneuvered his way through the traps and made his way across the yard to where Cheveyo stood. "I guess when the landlord said he would put out traps to catch the raccoon, he wasn't joking," Cheveyo remarked. "By the way, how's Lin? Is she still in a bad mood?" "Yes," Cash sighed, running a hand through his hair. "She's really upset right now. Yesterday, she lost her ring in the bathroom, and now she's saying the rest of her jewelry was taken from the bedroom."

Cheveyo looked at him with concern. "What? How could that happen? She was wearing all her jewelry all day long." "I don't know," Cash replied, his voice low and confused. "I don't know what's going on." Cash and Cheveyo walked over to join the rest of the group by the fire. As they approached, Cheveyo raised his voice to capture everyone's attention. "Good evening, everyone! Thank you for joining us once again on this lovely night. And now, let me share a Native American traditional ceremony."

A Native American friend of Cheveyo's began playing a deer-skinned drum, its rhythm deep and steady, while an older Native American man accompanied him on a flute. Cheveyo placed a bundle of dry sage into the fire, and a thick, aromatic smoke began to rise. "Smudging is a ceremony practiced by my ancestors and has been passed down through many generations," Cheveyo explained. "This smoke will cleanse your spirit and purify your minds."

A white plume of smoke rose into the air, and Cheveyo began to chant softly, his voice carrying with the breeze. He gestured for Cash and the others to join in. Dan and Ivy eagerly picked up instruments, joining the rhythm. Cheveyo pulled out a feather and a smudge bowl, carefully transferring the burning sage into it. The smoke curled from the bowl as he moved from person to person, guiding the smoke with the feather, purifying their minds, bodies, and souls. Cash sat on a log, watching as his friends danced around the fire. Their shadows stretched against the trees, moving like the spirits of ancestors long past. The embers crackled and drifted up into the night sky, blending with the rising smoke. Gary, an older man sitting near Cash, reached into his deerskin leather case and pulled out a wooden flute, its surface decorated with feathers. He began to play a soft, melodic tune. "Hey, Cash," Gary called out. "You want to try it?"

Cash carefully took the flute, feeling the smooth wood beneath his fingers. As he raised it to his lips, the music flowed effortlessly, a hauntingly beautiful Native American song. He played softly, his breath matching the rhythm of the fire. Gary watched him, nodding appreciatively. "Very nice! You've got a real natural musical talent there." "You think so?" Cash asked, surprised. "I know so," Gary replied with a smile. "I've been a musician all my life. And I can tell when someone's got the gift. Don't waste it."

Cash considered his words, nodding. "Thank you. That means a lot to me." Gary looked at him thoughtfully. "I want you to have this," he said, offering the flute to Cash. Cash hesitated, his fingers brushing over the flute. "Oh, I couldn't accept this. It's far too valuable." "It was a gift from my grandfather," Gary explained. "And now I want to give it to you. When I hear you play, the spirit of the flute comes alive. I would be honored if you'd accept it." "Are you sure..." Cash began, unsure. Gary nodded firmly. "Please, take it."

Cash held the flute in his hands, staring down at the intricate carvings. "Thank you," he said softly, the weight of the moment sinking in. Gary smiled at him. "It was meant to be." Cash stood there for a moment, watching Gary walk away, before his gaze fell to the flute again. For the first time, he realized just how much music meant to him. His hand brushed against the white business card in his pocket. It was from Linda. With a sudden resolve, Cash pulled it out and held it beside the flute. Slowly, he tossed the card into the fire, watching it curl and burn, the flames devouring the last remnants of his past.

Cash was finishing up the dishes when Cheveyo, Dan, and Ivy said their goodnights and went to bed. Lin emerged from the bedroom, her expression anxious. "I found some mouse traps under the sink," she said quietly, her hands nervously touching her earlobes. Cash looked at her, surprised. "Oh, yeah?" "My ears really hurt from these earrings, and I need to take them off," Lin explained. "But I want to make sure no one takes my last two pieces of jewelry. Can you help me?" Cash glanced at her diamond clip earrings, still sparkling in the dim light. "You don't have anything to worry about. Did you see all those traps outside?"

Lin looked at him, a worried frown on her face. "But there aren't any traps inside. I need you to set these mouse traps to protect my earrings." Reluctantly, Cash took the traps from her, and she grabbed a few cans of coffee. Together, they made their way to the master bedroom. Lin directed Cash to place the mouse traps on the nightstand. Once done, she removed her earrings, placing one on each trap with a devilish grin. "Whoever you are, you're not going to get away with it this time," she muttered under her breath. She closed the door securely and set the coffee cans on the nightstand. As she slid beneath the comforter, her eyes never left her precious earrings.

Cash turned to leave, noticing the coffee cans. "What are you doing with all that coffee?" Lin shushed him. "Go to sleep. I know what I'm doing." Cash frowned but said nothing, turning off the light as the moonlight filtered through the window, casting a pale glow over Lin's face. She reached for a can of coffee and took a gulp. Cash rolled over, covering his head with his pillow. An hour later, Lin had consumed two cans of coffee. Then another hour passed, and the remaining two cans disappeared. She began to nod off, sitting upright, her eyes growing heavy. She failed to notice that the cans were decaf. A shadowy figure appeared outside the window, lingering for a moment, before slipping silently toward the front of the cabin.

Wake-Up Call

The front door creaked open slowly, its hinges groaning in the quiet of the night. The Goblin's shadow stretched unnaturally across the living room floor as he slinked inside, his movements masked by the darkness. His loose-fitting, blood-red medieval cloak rippled behind him like a sinister flag, and his breath came in shallow bursts as he crept forward.

Cheveyo was oblivious, snoring on the sofa bed with his headset on, lost in a world of music or dreamless sleep. The Goblin's eyes narrowed as they fell upon the silver necklace that glittered faintly in the moonlight, resting around Cheveyo's neck. With a wicked grin, the Goblin moved closer, his footsteps barely making a sound on the creaky wooden floor. He noticed the feather—the one used in the sage ceremony—lying on the floor nearby. He picked it up with swift, careful fingers and hovered it near Cheveyo's exposed shoulder. Gently, he tickled the skin, causing Cheveyo to stir and roll over in his sleep. Seizing the opportunity, the Goblin snatched the necklace, slipping it into his pocket before quickly retreating.

The sound of a door creaking open in the guest bedroom made him freeze. Ivy stepped into the hallway, her footsteps soft as she walked toward the kitchen. The Goblin crouched low, ducking under the coffee table, watching her from the shadows. As Ivy poured herself a glass of water, the Goblin crept closer to the guest bedroom, his eyes flickering back and forth. With practiced speed, the Goblin darted into the room, unseen.

Dan lay sprawled across the lower bunk, his arm hanging off the edge of the bed. On his wrist, a shiny new gold Rolex gleamed in the low light. The Goblin's gaze fixed on the watch. His body tensed, and he moved quickly, climbing the ladder to remove the watch with deft fingers. The precious object slipped into his pocket without a sound. Just as he was about to leave, the door creaked again. Ivy, returning to her bed, was nearly at the top of the ladder when she froze, her eyes widening in horror. The Goblin leapt back, climbing the ladder to the top bunk, hiding behind the edge.

Ivy and the Goblin shrieked simultaneously. "Ahhh!" "Eeee!" Ivy tumbled backward, falling down the ladder with a thud. The Goblin slid down after her, darting for the living room, where he squeezed under the coffee table once more. Dan stirred, his eyes snapping open. He jumped out of the lower bunk. "Ivy, are you okay? What happened?" Ivy, shaking, with a small gash on her head managed to gasp, "I saw this creepy thing on top of my bed. It was furry, with big yellow eyes. It looked like a deformed monkey."

Cash and Lin were startled awake by the commotion, rushing into the guest bedroom to find Ivy sprawled on the floor, her face pale and wide-eyed. "What's going on in here? Are you guys okay?" Cash asked. Dan explained, "Ivy thinks she saw a deformed monkey in her bed." Lin raised an eyebrow. "Are you sure it wasn't just a nightmare?" Cash smirked. "Or maybe a raccoon... or a possum?" "No! It wasn't a raccoon or possum!" Ivy snapped. "It was an ugly, scary thing!" The Goblin, hidden beneath the coffee table, strained to listen. His eyes shifted toward the master bedroom door, now wide open. He was careful not to make a sound as he slipped toward the darkened doorway.

Inside the master bedroom, Cheveyo lay fast asleep, his headset still firmly in place, blocking out all the commotion from the rest of the house. The Goblin jumped onto the bed, his eyes scanning the nightstand. He spotted something—a set of keys and some loose change scattered carelessly. Reaching out with his long, spindly arm, he grabbed a couple of coins, his eyes narrowing with greedy satisfaction. He flicked them into the air, but not without triggering something. The traps on the nightstand snapped shut, the earrings flying into the air. In one swift motion, the Goblin leapt off the bed and snatched the earrings mid-flight, landing near Cash's nightstand. Without hesitation, he grabbed the keys and sprinted for the window. He threw it open with a quick motion, the cool night air rushing in as he made his escape. "Woohoo! Eeaaoo!" he yelled in triumph as he vanished into the night.

Dan, Ivy, Cash, and Lin paused in the living room, all of them hearing something—the sound of something large moving in the shadows. They turned toward each other, their faces filled with confusion and fear. "What was that?" Dan asked. Ivy's eyes widened. "It's that thing!"

Lin bolted for the door, heading toward the master bedroom, a sudden dread crawling up her spine. She stormed into the room, her eyes scanning the nightstand. Her heart sank when she saw the empty coffee cans strewn about, the mouse traps snapped shut without the earrings. "Noooo!" she gasped. Her gaze darted toward the open window, the curtains fluttering gently in the breeze. She poked her head out, frantically searching for any sign of the thief.

Cash stepped into the room, his eyes quickly searching for his keys, which were now gone. "Oh no...!" he muttered. The four of them hurried back into the living room, waking Cheveyo from his slumber. "My keys are gone... Is anyone else missing anything?" Cash asked. Dan's face fell. "My watch!" Cheveyo looked at them, his eyes wide. "My necklace is gone!" Lin's voice cracked as she spoke. "My earrings were stolen!" Ivy shrugged. "Well... at least my headache's gone..." Cash's expression darkened. "Alright, that's it. We need to talk to the landlord. Now!"

The Legend Unfolds

The night air was cold as Cash pounded on Barry's RV trailer door. Everyone stood tense and agitated, their frustration mounting. The light above the door flickered on, casting a harsh green glow on their faces. Through the peephole, Barry's tired eyes met theirs. He opened the door slowly, his hair a mess, his robe inside out, clearly caught off guard. "Barry, someone just broke in again!" Cash's voice was sharp, full of urgency. "All of our valuables are gone, Ivy's hurt, and my car keys are missing! What's going on around here?"

Barry stared at them, his face heavy with exhaustion. After a long moment, he sighed. "Okay, come in... I can explain everything if you come inside." He opened the door wider, letting them in. But before they stepped through, he glanced outside, scanning the darkness, as if expecting something to jump out at him. He locked the door behind them with a long, deliberate click. Inside, the RV was a chaotic mix of old books, ancient artifacts, and maps littered with Barry's scribbled notes. The air smelled musty, as though the walls themselves had been soaked in time. "Come in and sit down," Barry muttered, moving toward the small dining table. Cash, Cheveyo, Dan, and Ivy took their seats. Dan and Ivy sat side by side, while Cheveyo and Cash sat on the opposite side. Barry grabbed a small stool and gestured for Lin to sit at the end.

Without saying much, Barry shuffled into the kitchen area and poured himself a cup of sake. The room fell into a thick silence as he mumbled to himself. "I should've seen this coming... That obnoxious girl and all her shiny jewelry..." Barry drank down the sake quickly, as though trying to calm his nerves. Everyone stared at him, waiting for an explanation. "Oh, pardon me," he said, suddenly remembering them. "Let me make some for you, too."

He grabbed more cups and filled them, spilling some sake across the counter in the process. He brought the cups to the table, handing each person one with a distracted look. Cash's eyes wandered to a shelf above the dining table, where several photos of a much younger Barry in the gold mines stared back at them. "A long time ago," Barry began, his voice quiet but laced with bitterness, "I fell in love with a girl from a wealthy family. Her father could never accept me because I didn't have a penny to my name."

A shadow passed over his face, and he took another long swig of sake. "One day, I saw a sign—miners needed to work the gold mines. I thought... if I was lucky enough to find some gold, maybe I could sneak some out and make a fortune. Maybe I'd finally be able to go after that girl I was so madly in love with."

The group listened, captivated by his story. "So ten long years went by, but I never managed to sneak anything out," Barry continued. "Then the company went bankrupt. There was no more gold in the mountain. On that last day, I saw something glimmering deep in the mine—something that caught my eye." Barry abruptly stood, turning toward his bedroom. He ducked under the Japanese drapes, and they could hear him rummaging around. Moments later, he emerged, holding something covered in a burgundy cloth. With a flourish, he pulled it off, revealing a golden sword with a German inscription etched into its blade. "This cursed thing," Barry said, setting it down in the middle of the table. The group leaned forward, mesmerized by the sword's gleaming surface. "I know who took your jewelry," Barry added, his voice dropping. Lin's brow furrowed. "Then, tell us."

Barry hesitated, the weight of his words pressing down on him. Everyone held their breath. "The Goblin," Barry said finally, his voice barely above a whisper. The silence in the RV was palpable. The group exchanged confused glances, processing what they'd just heard. "What?!" Lin exclaimed, unable to believe it. "The Goblin took it all," Barry repeated, his posture relaxing slightly, as if unloading a burden. He sipped from his cup again, his eyes distant. "This is crazy! I'm calling the police!" Lin snapped, already pulling out her phone. "You can't," Dan reminded her. "There's no reception, remember?"

Barry's gaze turned cold. "You're the one who spit the gum in his bowl... That's what started it all." Cash's brow furrowed. "Wait a minute, what bowl?" Barry took a deep breath, clearly irritated. "I always leave a bowl of warm milk out for the Goblin every night. He's very particular about it... that nasty little devil." The group stared at him, trying to comprehend his words. "I've been doing it for almost 200 years," Barry added, his voice heavy with regret. Cheveyo leaned forward, his eyes narrowing in thought. "Wait a minute... My grandfather used to speak of this legend..."

Barry poured himself more sake, taking a long gulp. "Stories about a sword," Cheveyo continued, his voice laced with awe. "It goes back centuries." He couldn't tear his eyes away from the golden sword as he spoke. "The legend is about a miner who found a golden sword deep in the mines of Gold Mountain. They say his life was extended, but at a cost... There's an inscription on the sword that explains the curse." Cheveyo pointed to the words etched into the blade. "I think this is in German. Can anyone read German?" Lin rolled her eyes, pretending she hadn't heard him. Cash turned to her. "Lin can..."

Everyone's attention shifted to Lin, who sighed, reluctant but unable to ignore them. She leaned over the table and squinted at the inscription. *"I feed on greed, I feast on fear, Bound to you, I always near. Wash me pure, and break my curse, Or live in shadows, for far worse."*

Barry's eyes flickered to his hands, and Lin noticed a scar on his fingertip. As she looked, Barry clenched his fist tightly. Cheveyo raised an eyebrow. "And if the legend is true, that would make you nearly 200 years old." Everyone looked at Barry. He smiled sheepishly, a slight glint in his eyes. "Er, uh... I look pretty good for my age, right?" Barry chuckled awkwardly. "Well, if you want your stuff back, you're going to need this." He reached up to a shelf and pulled out a keychain, the ancient keys clinking together. He took a large, rusted medieval-looking key from the ring and examined it carefully before handing it to Cash. "This key opens the door to the Goblin's lair, deep in the mine," Barry said. "Everything the Goblin takes, it's all in that one cave. That's where he keeps his stolen treasures."

Cash's face hardened. "Can you lead us there?" Barry shook his head, a bitter laugh escaping his lips. "I'm too old to hike all the way up there. Besides, I wouldn't fit through his door anyway. He's a tiny little sucker." Cheveyo's expression turned serious. "But there are many mines up there. How will we know which is the right one?" "Follow the North Star," Barry said, his voice low and sure. "It'll lead you right there. But you need to get there by midnight. When the full moon shines through the trees, you'll see the shape of a Goblin pointing directly to the right cave."

Cash checked his watch. "We should go now! It's almost midnight!" Lin crossed her arms, her skepticism evident. "You've got to be kidding me. You actually believe this? We could all die up there!" Barry shot her a look. "Don't you want your precious jewelry back?" Lin hesitated, her mind a swirl of conflicting thoughts. "Take the key," Barry urged, his tone softer. "Get your stuff back... and go home." Dan scoffed. "That simple, huh? Just open the door, grab our stuff, and walk out?" Barry's expression turned grim. "I didn't say it was simple... If the Goblin catches you trying to steal his treasure..." Lin and Ivy exchanged a worried look. "What happens?" Cash asked, his voice tense. Barry leaned back, his eyes narrowing. "You don't want to know. Trust me. It'll be Hell on Earth, that's for sure."

With that, Barry grabbed Lin's sake cup and downed it in one go. "We gotta go if we're gonna make it in time," Cash said, standing quickly. Everyone scrambled to their feet, preparing to leave. Barry threw up a hand. "Wait! One more thing..." Cash turned, raising an eyebrow. "What? Do we need to bring milk?" Barry shook his head, his expression serious. "It's too late for that... Only take what is yours. Nothing more." Cash nodded, and with that, they rushed out of the RV, leaving Barry standing behind, holding his sake cup, his eyes lingering on the empty doorway. "I can't believe we're actually doing this..." Lin muttered, following reluctantly behind her friends.

Scaling the Mountain

The full moon bathed the lake in a silvery glow, its reflection dancing across the water. The only sound was the soft splash of paddles as Dan and Cheveyo steered their canoe along the shoreline. Cash checked his watch, then surveyed the mountain looming ahead. Lin and Ivy huddled together, exchanging nervous glances. "We should've taken the other boat," Lin said, her voice tight with unease. Cheveyo shook his head. "That would've been too loud. We need to be as quiet as possible." He pointed up at the mountain. "Once we get there, we have to stay together. No one can be left behind." "I'm not going inside the mine," Lin declared, crossing her arms over her chest. Cash shot her a tired look. "Lin..." "I'll wait outside," Lin interrupted, her voice firm. Cash had no patience left to argue. He glanced back at the others, the weight of the decision hanging heavy in the air. "It's OK, Cash," Dan said, sensing the tension. "We need someone outside anyway, in case something goes wrong. Lin can run for help."

Cheveyo tied the canoe to a narrow dock. One by one, they climbed out, the creaking wood under their feet adding to the eerie quiet of the night. Cash reached for Lin's hand, but she pulled away and walked ahead. "Which way should we go?" Lin asked, her voice laced with anxiety. "Follow the North Star," Cheveyo replied, pointing up at the bright, steady star overhead. Beneath it, a trail wound its way up the mountain. They trudged onward, the steep canyon walls rising on either side. The moonlight filtered through the trees, lighting their path. After some time, the trail split in two directions. "Which way?" Cash asked, pausing at the fork. Cheveyo knelt down, studying the sky, his eyes returning to the North Star. It pointed directly between the two paths. Puzzled, Cheveyo pushed through the shrubs, revealing a hidden trail. "This way," he said, flashing a grin at the others, urging them to follow. They continued along the narrow path, eventually coming to a rickety wooden bridge that creaked under their weight. It was old—used to transport supplies to the mines long before the Civil War. They crossed slowly, the wood groaning beneath them. Lin, who had been trailing behind, stepped too quickly and her foot went through one of the loose boards. "Ahhh!" Lin screamed, her body jerking downward.

Cash reacted instinctively, grabbing her wrist to stop her from falling completely. But she was too heavy to lift on his own. Ivy reached out to grab Cash, and Dan quickly joined in, pulling on Ivy to steady the situation. Cheveyo grabbed onto Dan, strengthening the chain of hands. "On three," Cheveyo grunted, his muscles straining. "We pull together. One, two, three, pull!" With a collective heave, they managed to pull Lin back onto the bridge, but she staggered back angrily. "Ahhh! Cash, you fool!" Lin shouted. "I'm done with you! You're so stupid. You're gonna get us all killed. I shouldn't have come on this stupid trip with you and your stupid friends. When we get back, you're out of my house! You can live on the street with the rats!"

Cash stood there, stunned, taking the abuse in silence. Lin stormed past him, her anger propelling her forward without a backward glance. Cheveyo was the first to break the tension. "We're almost there, but we're running out of time. Let's go, guys!" He pushed ahead, his urgency pushing them all forward. They reached the foot of the mountain, and the entrance to the mines loomed in the distance, dark and foreboding. There were at least a dozen mines cut into the mountain, all looking identical. "Which one could it be?" Ivy asked, peering around. "There are so many," Dan added. "And they all look the same." Cash glanced down at his watch—11:59 PM. He and Cheveyo exchanged a glance, each hoping for some sign. Then, a cold breeze brushed the back of Cash's neck. He turned, eyes narrowing, toward an old, twisted pine tree standing on the edge of the clearing. As the moonlight filtered through its branches, a shadow stretched out across the ground.

Cheveyo took a step forward, squinting at the shadow. "This doesn't look like a Goblin," he muttered. "It's just a blob." Cash frowned, feeling the unease deep in his chest. He studied the shadow again, watching as it seemed to shift, almost as if alive. And then, from the blob, something began to emerge—an arm, stretching out. Cash's stomach twisted. The shadow wasn't just a blob—it belonged to Lin. He stepped toward her and gave her a nudge to move her out of the way. "Lin, you're blocking the shadow," Cash said, his voice tense.

As Lin stepped aside, the shadow separated, and a new, more distinct shape emerged. The shadow of a Goblin, its grotesque outline casting an ominous presence. Ivy gasped, her hand clutching Dan's arm. "Ahhh!" Ivy cried out, her voice high and sharp with fear. The wind picked up, a cold, biting gust scattering dust and dead leaves. Everyone shivered as the shadow of the Goblin trembled in the wind. Then, Cheveyo pointed. "Over there! It's that one!"

The Forbidden Mine

They hurried toward the mine entrance, their breath coming in short, nervous bursts. The shadow had led them here, but now that they stood before it, hesitation set in. The opening was small—just big enough to crawl through. Cash and Cheveyo exchanged a glance before kneeling down. Without a word, they switched on their flashlights and crawled inside, their beams slicing through the darkness. Dan and Ivy followed close behind, their movements careful, their breathing shallow.

The tunnel was tight at first, the damp earth pressing in around them. But as they moved forward, the space gradually widened, allowing them to rise to their feet. The air was thick, heavy with dust and something else—something old. Back at the entrance, Lin lingered. She hesitated, peering inside, her fingers gripping the rough edges of the opening. Cash turned back and spotted her silhouette outlined against the night. "C'mon, Lin!" he called. Lin shook her head. "I'm not going in there."

She stepped back and settled onto a rock beside the mine's entrance, arms crossed tightly over her chest. Cash sighed, shifting his weight. "Well, if you're not coming with us, can you at least keep a lookout? If something happens—if you think we're in danger—give us a warning. Can you do that?" Lin's expression flickered between annoyance and fear. She didn't want to be left alone out here, but the thought of going inside was worse. "Yeah, sure," she muttered. "I can do that." She watched as their flashlight beams bobbed and flickered, growing dimmer as they disappeared deeper into the mine.

Cheveyo led the way into the mine, his flashlight cutting through the suffocating darkness. Cash, Dan, and Ivy followed closely behind, their footsteps echoing against the damp stone walls. The tunnel soon split into three separate paths, each yawning open like a waiting mouth. Cash exhaled sharply. "Oh, no! Which way, Cheveyo?" Without answering, Cheveyo crouched, sweeping his flashlight across the ground in front of each tunnel. His sharp eyes caught something—strange little footprints pressed into the dirt, leading toward the passage on the right. "See that?" he murmured. "This way. But be as quiet as possible. I think we're getting close."

They tightened their formation, moving together as they entered the passage. Small dark alcoves punctuated the walls of the mine, each one a pocket of unknown horrors. As they passed one of them, Ivy stopped short, her body going rigid. Dan noticed immediately. "What's wrong?" She pointed a trembling finger at the hole. Without hesitation, Dan raised his flashlight. A split second later, a rat lunged out, claws scrambling for purchase as it landed on Dan's arm. "Ahhh! Ahhhh!" Dan yelled, flailing. He swung his flashlight, knocking the rat off. It hit the ground with a shriek before scurrying away into the abyss. Dan's breath came in ragged gasps as Ivy clung to him, her face buried in his shoulder. "Keep it down, guys," Cash whispered harshly. "Let's keep moving."

Cheveyo signaled them forward with a quick flick of his light. The deeper they went, the thicker the air became. A fine mist curled around their ankles, swirling with each cautious step. Then, a sound—a soft crunch beneath their boots. Ivy swallowed. "Do you hear that?" "Hear what?" Dan asked, though he had started to notice it too. Cheveyo's flashlight caught movement—a large bug skittering along the wall before disappearing into the fog. Something about it made his stomach tighten. He crouched, brushing his hand through the mist to clear it. What he uncovered sent a chill through his bones.

Tiny animal skeletons, hundreds of them, brittle and half-buried in layers of decay. And crawling over them, countless hungry insects. Cheveyo muttered under his breath, "I thought he liked milk…" Ivy turned toward him. "What did you say?" He quickly straightened, masking his unease. "Nothing… let's keep moving." The mist rose higher, swirling around their waists. Then—another noise. A soft, rhythmic flapping in the distance. Cash tensed. "See anything?"

Cheveyo swept his light ahead, but the thick fog swallowed it whole. Suddenly, Ivy stumbled, instinctively reaching out to steady herself against the wall. Her fingers met something wet and sticky. "Eww!! What is this?!" Before anyone could react, a swarm of bats exploded from the mist, their high-pitched screeches piercing the silence. Cheveyo and Cash ducked, arms shielding their heads. One of the bats struck Ivy, sending her toppling backward.

As she hit the ground, the fog momentarily parted—revealing the skeletal remains littering the mine floor. Ivy's scream shattered the air. Far away, in the dense forest beyond the mine, something heard her. The Goblin. Its ears twitched, catching the sound like a predator honing in on its prey. With an unnatural speed, it lunged through the underbrush, heading toward the mountain. Back inside the mine, Dan knelt beside Ivy, his hands hovering near her torn jeans. Blood seeped from a fresh gash on her knee.

Cheveyo's jaw clenched. "Dan, you gotta get Ivy outta here!" Dan nodded, already moving. "Ivy, give me your arm." She winced as he helped her up, draping her arm over his shoulders. Together, they retraced their steps, disappearing into the shadows, leaving only two behind. Cash turned to Cheveyo, gripping his flashlight tighter. "Now it's up to you and me, buddy." They pressed forward, deeper into the tunnel. The walls became tangled with thick tree roots, hanging like skeletal fingers from the ceiling. Webs stretched across their path, clinging to their skin as they forced their way through. Then—they stopped. The tunnel ended. Before them stood a small, warped green door, carved from splintered wood. The handle, rusted and corroded, seemed untouched for centuries. Strange, ancient symbols covered its surface, their meaning lost to time. Cash swallowed hard. "This is it." The Goblin's lair.

The Green Door

The key was cold in Cash's hand as he quickly fumbled it from his pocket and handed it over to Cheveyo. The old, rusty lock resisted at first, but after a few moments of fiddling and the sound of metal scraping against metal, Cheveyo's efforts were rewarded. The key finally turned with a low click. Cheveyo grunted as he shoved against the door, which was heavier than it had first seemed. It creaked and groaned under the pressure. Cash, standing beside him, leaned into it with his shoulder. Together, they pushed harder, and with a final strained squeak from the hinges, the door slowly inched open.

The air that poured out from the cave was cool, and the faint scent of earth lingered. As the door creaked open, the beam of their flashlights revealed the treasure before them. Gold coins, sparkling gems, diamonds, and glistening objects of all kinds shimmered in the dim light. "Whoa!" Cash breathed out, the wonder in his voice thick. His heart raced as his eyes scanned the treasure that seemed to stretch on forever. "C'mon, let's find our stuff and get outta here!" Cheveyo urged, his voice low but with excitement bubbling underneath.

Cash nodded, his feet already moving forward as they both began sifting through the mounds of treasure. Their flashlights bounced off golden crowns, ruby-encrusted rings, and diamond necklaces, reflecting the light back like a million tiny stars. It wasn't long before Lin, who had evidently followed them into the cave, appeared in the doorway. Her eyes went wide, and a greedy, almost giddy smile spread across her face. "Oh, my gosh! Look at all this gold!" Lin gasped, stepping forward. Her voice trembled with excitement as she walked past Cash and Cheveyo. "Diamonds, rubies… This place is better than Tiffany's!" "Don't touch anything!" Cash snapped, his tone sharp. "Remember what the Landlord said—only take what belongs to you!"

Lin didn't listen. Instead, she let out a scoff and began shoving gems into her pockets. Cash could only watch in frustration. "I'm done with you!" Lin shot back, not bothering to glance at him. Cash shook his head, but his attention was already drawn to a small shelf near the Goblin's bed. It was lined with keys, and Cash's heart skipped a beat. There they were. His keys. He hurried over, pushing past the glittering treasure, and grabbed the set, a relieved sigh escaping him. "I found my keys! Let's get out of here!" he called out, turning toward Cheveyo.

Cheveyo, still sifting through the gold, suddenly froze. His light landed on something hanging on the wall—a glimmering Native American silver necklace. His face lit up with recognition. "I've got my necklace," he grinned, grabbing it from the wall. Meanwhile, Lin was still stuffing her pockets with gold when something else caught her eye. In the corner of the room, a gold-colored satchel lay waiting. She couldn't resist. With a greedy grin, she picked it up and began filling it. "Lin, we gotta go!" Cash urged, shining his light around to make sure they weren't missing anything else.

His beam landed on something resting on top of a small, weathered animal skull—a gold Rolex. Cash scooped it up. "This belongs to Dan!" he muttered, then tossed it to Cheveyo. "Let's move!" Cheveyo urged, and Lin zipped her satchel shut, finally following them. Just before she reached the exit, Lin's eyes flashed with desire. Hanging from the wall was a gold necklace, its chain heavy with precious gems. She couldn't resist. She grabbed it and slipped it over her head, the weight of the gold heavy around her neck.

Cash barely spared her a glance as they made their way back to the mine's entrance. Once outside, the five of them regrouped. Cash tossed Dan the watch. "Let's get outta here before the Goblin shows up!" Cash said, his voice tight with urgency. They turned and began sprinting down the mountain, the full moon casting a cold silver light over the still lake below. As they ran, the distant sound of something moving through the forest reached their ears. The Goblin was coming.

Back in the mine, the Goblin burst through the cave entrance, his eyes narrowing as he saw the open green door. His heart raced as he stepped forward, his hands clenched into fists. His precious gold was missing. With a snarl, he turned and dashed back into the darkness, racing after the thieves who had dared to steal from him.

The Chase

A cold wind whipped through the mountain, carrying with it a foreboding sense of dread. High above the valley, perched on the jagged rocks of the old mine, the Goblin—pale and twisted—scrambled to the edge, his eyes scanning the shadows. Beneath him, five figures sprinted down the winding path toward the distant lake, their silhouettes barely visible against the dark landscape.

With a shriek that echoed through the trees, the Goblin raised his head and called out into the night, the sound haunting and primal. "AHHHHKKK!" The figures below paused, halting in their tracks as the call reverberated through the air. They turned, eyes wide with fear, exchanging silent glances. They knew what was coming. Cash, the bravest of the group, felt his heart race. They'd come so far—too far to turn back now—but he knew the Goblin was close, tracking them down with an unrelenting fury.

The Goblin tilted his head, sniffing the air, and then darted down the mountain, his movements swift and animalistic. He could smell their fear, the scent of panic rising from their skin, and he pursued it relentlessly. They reached the edge of the lake, panting, their breath misting in the cold air. The narrow dock stretched out before them, and the small canoe bobbed gently in the water. "We're almost there!" Cheveyo called out, glancing nervously over his shoulder. "We couldn't have made it this far without you, buddy!" Cash said, clapping Cheveyo on the back. "Don't thank me yet. We're not home free."

Dan and Ivy scrambled into the canoe first, their movements frantic. Cheveyo helped Cash into the boat, his hands trembling. Lin, however, wasn't done. She appeared behind them, holding the heavy satchel filled with the Goblin's cursed treasure. "No, Lin! You can't bring that!" Cash protested. "If you do, the Goblin will come after us!" Lin shot him a defiant look, her jaw set. "Quiet, Cash! I'm not leaving this behind." With a determined cry, Lin jumped into the canoe, still clutching the satchel. The canoe tipped, and the heavy bag slipped from her grasp, plunging into the water. The canoe flipped over, sending them all tumbling into the cold lake. "Noooo!! Cash, you idiot! This is all your fault!!" Lin's voice rang out from the water as she surfaced, furious and soaked.

Cash's chest tightened with guilt as the others swam toward the dock. Lin, her eyes wild with rage, clung to a wooden post, staring down into the depths of the lake, searching for the satchel that was now lost forever. "Lin, let it go! Forget about the gold! It's not worth it!" Cash pleaded, reaching for her. "Stupid!" Lin snapped, still glaring at him. "What are you going to do with your life? Be a musician? You'll never make it! I saw you burn that business card last night. I worked so hard to get that for you. You had a golden opportunity, and you threw it away. I'm done with you!" With those final words, Lin dived back into the water, disappearing beneath the surface. Cash's heart sank as he watched her disappear, but there was no time to linger. He turned away and joined the others, their eyes filled with shared urgency.

Dan, Ivy, Cheveyo, and Cash ran along the shoreline, desperately searching for another boat. But there was nothing. Cheveyo glanced toward the mountain. "Oh no…" His voice was barely a whisper. He waved frantically at the others. "Into the forest, quick! Follow me!" Without hesitation, they darted into the dense woods, Cheveyo leading the way. The trees loomed above them like ancient sentinels, and the underbrush crackled beneath their feet as they ran. Cheveyo led them with practiced ease, but Cash could hear the sound of footsteps pounding behind them—too close, too fast.

They reached a small creek, splashing through the cold water as they crossed to the other side. Suddenly, Cheveyo stopped. "I saw him," he whispered. Cash froze, looking back toward the lake. He could see nothing, but the hairs on the back of his neck stood on end. The Goblin reached the shore, his yellow eyes scanning the water. Lin was still swimming, her frantic movements a clear sign of her obsession with the lost satchel. The Goblin sniffed the air, his senses sharpened. He could smell the others in the forest. He turned toward the woods, his gaze narrowing. "*Heh heh heh,*" the Goblin cackled, before charging into the forest to continue his pursuit.

The Goblin's presence was undeniable now. His pace was relentless, the sound of his footfalls echoing through the trees. Cheveyo, Cash, Dan, and Ivy pushed forward, desperation lending them speed. Ivy glanced behind her, her breath catching in her throat. "He's coming!" she screamed. "Keep running!" Cheveyo urged. They picked up their pace, but Ivy, in her panic, stumbled over a log. As she fell, Dan tripped over her, cutting his leg on the rough bark. "We've got to keep going!" Cheveyo shouted, as Cash and Cheveyo helped Dan to his feet.

The cabin was just ahead, its silhouette barely visible in the distance. They were almost there. But not fast enough. Ivy burst through the front door and rushed to the kitchen, grabbing a knife, while Cheveyo and Cash dragged Dan inside, throwing him onto the sofa bed. Cheveyo glanced out the window. "He's coming!" He bolted to the door, slamming it shut and locking it with a deadbolt just as the Goblin's massive frame collided with it, rattling the wood. "Lock the windows!" Cheveyo shouted. Cash and Ivy scrambled around the cabin, sealing every opening they could find. Dan collapsed onto the couch, his leg bleeding. Ivy grabbed the first aid kit from the bathroom and began tending to his wound. But then the lights went out. "What happened?" Cash asked, his voice tight with panic.

The living room was bathed in the eerie glow of moonlight, casting long twisted shadows across the floor. Cash approached the window, scanning the night for any sign of the Goblin's approach. "We need to block the door," Cheveyo said, turning to Cash. Together, they moved the sofa bed in front of the door, barricading it as best they could. Then, a sound came from the chimney—a strange, scratching noise, as though something was crawling through it. Dust and soot spilled out from the fireplace. "Cash, quick! Get a fire going!" Cheveyo urged.

Cash grabbed some newspaper and began crumpling it, while Cheveyo searched for matches. But the box was empty. "We need a match!" Cash cried. Dan, wincing in pain, reached into his pocket and pulled out a small book of matches. There were only three left. "Cash!" Dan called, tossing the book over to Cash. With trembling hands, Cash struck the first match—nothing. The Goblin's skeletal fingers began to emerge from the fireplace. "Ivy, get back!" Cheveyo warned. The second match was a dud too. But the third... the third lit, and the flame caught. Fire spread quickly, forcing the Goblin to retreat. He screeched in fury, but they had bought themselves a little more time.

Hide and Seek

Cheveyo grabbed two kitchen knives and slid one across the counter to Cash. Cash eyed the knife skeptically. "This is a cake knife!" he muttered, picking it up and holding it at arm's length. Cheveyo gave a small smirk. "Looks like mine's a butter knife," he said, showing off his own. Both men turned to Ivy, whose hand was wrapped tightly around a much more threatening sharp kitchen knife. She glared at them both, warning them with her eyes. "Don't even think about it," Ivy growled. The Goblin erupted from the smoke-filled chimney, his cloak aflame, tumbling violently to the ground with a series of painful coughs.

The Goblin rolled across the ground, desperately trying to extinguish the flames licking at his cloak. His scream, sharp and guttural, shattered the night air. "Eeeeaaaooo!!!" The sound sent nearby animals scrambling for cover. With fury in his eyes, the Goblin surged to his feet and charged toward the back door, ramming into it with the force of a battering ram.

The back door rattled violently, as if struck by a bull. The noise made everyone jump, retreating from the kitchen door in fear. Ivy knelt beside Dan, her hand resting gently on his arm as he wrapped an arm around her protectively. Cheveyo, his voice tight with urgency, turned to them. "Dan, Ivy, get to the bedroom and lock the door behind you!" he ordered. "If the Goblin makes it inside, jump out the window and run!" Ivy helped Dan to his feet, guiding him toward the bedroom. The door slammed shut behind them.

Cash turned back toward the kitchen door, cake knife still in hand, ready to defend them. Cheveyo muttered, a grim disbelief in his voice. "I never thought my grandpa's stories were true." Suddenly, a rock smashed through the small kitchen window. The Goblin's grotesque hand reached through the shattered glass, fumbling for the latch. Cash reacted immediately, grabbing the iron poker from the fireplace, running to the window, and stabbing the Goblin's hand with all his strength.

The Goblin shrieked in pain. "EEEEOOOAA!!!!" Cheveyo laughed, a sound full of dark satisfaction. "Hah! You didn't see that one coming, did you, you nasty little toad!" The Goblin, undeterred, began circling the perimeter of the cabin, trying every window and door, but finding them all secured. Meanwhile, Dan and Ivy heard a faint shadow outside their bedroom window, a tug on the latch. Cash noticed the fire in the chimney sputtering to an almost invisible glow, and then—just as quickly—the chimney rattled. A dark shape leapt from it, extinguishing the last remnants of the fire in a violent, explosive rush. The force sent ash scattering everywhere.

Smoke began to billow into the cabin as Cash and Cheveyo saw the Goblin running across the floor, disappearing into the shadows. "Heeehhehhehee." The Goblin's eerie laughter echoed through the room. "Oh no," Cheveyo said, his voice full of dread. "He's inside!" Cash swung the poker wildly, trying to clear a path through the smoke. The Goblin, faster than either of them could react, lunged at Cheveyo, sinking razor-sharp teeth into his ankle.

Cheveyo cried out. "Ahhhh! He bit my ankle!" Cash spun around, swinging the poker at the Goblin's retreating form, narrowly missing him as the creature sprang onto the bookshelf behind Cheveyo. Cash pointed urgently. "Behind you!" Cheveyo barely had time to move before Cash swung the poker at the Goblin, missing and smashing the bookshelf instead. Each time Cash swung, the Goblin danced away, leaving destruction in his wake. "Hehehheeeeeeh!" Inside the bedroom, Dan and Ivy could hear the chaos outside. Ivy pressed her ear to the door, listening closely. "Oh my gosh, it got inside!" she whispered, eyes wide with fear. "Quick! Block the door!" Dan urged.

They rushed to the dresser, dragging it across the room and wedging it against the door just as the sound of the Goblin's claws scratching at the walls grew louder. Cheveyo watched with growing frustration as the Goblin scurried about the room, evading every blow Cash aimed at him. Meanwhile, the cabin was being demolished with every swing. Cheveyo's gaze flicked upward. He saw the ceiling fan and, in a moment of inspiration, cracked open the windows and flipped the fan switch. The fan roared to life, clearing the smoke from the room.

The Goblin jumped onto the coffee table, a wicked grin spreading across his twisted face. Cash hurled the poker at him in desperation, but the Goblin ducked effortlessly, pulling a rusted medieval dagger from behind his back. "Where's my Gold?" the Goblin hissed, his eyes glowing with malice. Cheveyo and Cash scrambled toward the master bedroom door, but before they could reach it, the Goblin snapped his fingers, and the door slammed shut, locking itself. "Guys! Guys! Let us in!" Cheveyo shouted, banging on the door with all his might. Cash followed suit. "It's us! It's us! Let us in! Let us in!" But the Goblin, swift as a shadow, moved closer, stalking toward them, knife gleaming in the dim light.

Ivy and Dan quickly pulled the dresser away from the door at the sound of Cheveyo and Cash's frantic shouts. They let the two men in and slammed the door shut, pushing the dresser back into place. Exhausted, Cash and Cheveyo slid down to the floor, backs resting against the dresser. A sharp splintering sound cut through the air. A knife slid through the door, dangerously close to Cash's head. Dan and Ivy recoiled as they saw the Goblin's menacing smile peeking through the hole. "Block the door!" Cheveyo urged, his voice tight with fear.

Cash and Cheveyo turned around, using all their strength to push the dresser back against the door. But the Goblin was relentless. He stabbed again, the blade puncturing the wood with force, this time only inches from Cheveyo's side. The doorknob trembled. Slowly, it twisted, turning as though controlled by unseen hands. Dan's eyes widened. "I don't know how much longer I can hold this doorknob!" he said, his voice strained.

Dan braced himself against the dresser, his muscles straining as he fought to keep the door shut. But the Goblin was impossibly strong—stronger than the three of them combined. The door creaked open, inch by inch, its rusty hinges groaning under the pressure. Ivy, seeing their struggle, rushed to their side. She grabbed the corner of the dresser and pushed with all her strength. The Goblin snarled on the other side, its twisted fingers curling around the edge of the door.

Cheveyo's eyes darted to the nightstand where a small silver lighter slid off the surface, hitting the floor just beyond reach. His heart pounded. Then, something else caught his eye—a can of hairspray perched on the nightstand. "Ivy! Grab that hairspray and throw it to Cash!" Cheveyo shouted. Ivy stretched, her fingertips barely brushing the can. With a final nudge, she knocked it into her grasp, then tossed it toward Cash, who caught it just as Cheveyo lunged for the lighter.

Their eyes met for a brief moment. No words were needed—they both knew what to do.

The dresser shuddered as the Goblin forced the door wider. The creature's grotesque head pushed through the gap, its dark, hollow eyes glinting with malice. "I got it!" Cheveyo cried, flicking the lighter to life. Cash aimed the hairspray directly at the Goblin's face. The moment the mist shot out, Cheveyo brought the lighter close. A sudden roar of fire erupted, the flames swallowing the Goblin's twisted features.

The creature let out a horrific scream, its face burning, its clawed hands slapping wildly at the flames. It reeled backward, its body convulsing as it scrambled up the wall. Then, with unnatural speed, it staggered in circles across the ceiling, screeching in agony. "AAAiiiiiyow!" it howled, its voice echoing through the house. Wasting no time, Cash and Cheveyo shoved the door shut. Cash turned the lock, and together, they heaved the dresser back into place. For a moment, all was still—except for the Goblin's distant wails. Their chests heaved, their bodies trembling from the effort.

The Goblin's Fury

The Goblin scuttled down the hallway, his body twisted unnaturally as he moved upside-down along the ceiling. His charred face twitched with rage, his burnt eyebrows barely framing the gleam of his wild, black eyes. Then, he stopped—his gaze locking onto the open doorway of the bathroom. Without hesitation, he sprang forward, flipping midair as he plunged his face into the toilet bowl. A grotesque hissing sound filled the air, a sickening mix of steam and guttural groans. Smoke curled from the water as his blistered skin sizzled. "Mmmrrrgggghhh!" the Goblin grumbled, lifting his head. Droplets of water dripped from his scorched face. He touched his raw, stinging flesh and winced as steam hissed from his pores. His once-stringy beard was now a brittle mess of burnt stubble.

But his pain only fueled his rage. In the guest bedroom, Cash and Cheveyo shoved the heavy bunk bed against the dresser. Their breath came fast, sweat beading on their foreheads. Then—footsteps. Fast. Small. Terrifying. The Goblin was coming. A sudden *thud* hit the door, rattling it in its frame. Then another. Then another. The Goblin struck again and again, the wood splintering under his relentless assault. Then, the knife.

Its jagged blade punched through the door, slashing wildly. Shreds of wood fell away with each rapid, merciless strike. Everyone stumbled back. "Now what?" Dan gasped, eyes darting for an escape. "The window!" Cheveyo shouted. "It's our only chance!"

With no time to hesitate, he threw it open. The cold night air rushed in as they scrambled toward their only way out. But just as they climbed through, a new sound rang through the cabin— Banging. From the front door. Lin stood on the cabin's porch, her boot slamming into the door over and over again. Her voice rang out, high-pitched and furious. "Let me in, Cash! I wanna go home *right now!*" she screamed, fists pounding against the wood. "Because of *you,* I lost my ring, the rest of my jewelry, *and* all my gold! We are done, done, *done!*"

Just as the Goblin raised his knife for another strike at the bedroom door, he froze. His ears twitched. His grip tightened around the knife's handle, his nostrils flaring. Gold. The unmistakable, alluring sound of metal rubbing against metal. Slowly, he turned. Through the glass in the center of the front door, he saw it—a glint of gold dangling from Lin's neck. His necklace. *His.* A fire lit behind his eyes, a rage deeper than before.

With a furious screech, the Goblin spun around and sprinted toward the front of the house. His clawed feet pounded against the wooden floor as he leapt onto the sofa bed, his bony frame coiling like a spring. Then—he launched. The force of his scrawny legs sent him soaring through the air, his body aimed straight for the front door. With an earsplitting crash, the door exploded off its hinges, the impact sending it flying forward—slamming directly into Lin.

The force of the impact sent Lin flying backward. She hit the ground hard, her skull cracking against the dirt with a dull *thud.* Her body went limp, sprawled across the earth, her breath silent. The Goblin scrambled toward her, his clawed fingers reaching greedily for the gold necklace still looped around her throat. With a sharp tug, he yanked it free and held it up to the moonlight. His lips curled in delight before his eyes flicked back to Lin's unconscious face.

He leaned in, sniffing her. His nostrils flared. "Yewww! Yewwwk!" he gagged, recoiling in disgust. From around the corner of the cabin, the others approached cautiously, drawn by the sound of the door crashing open. Cash led the way, Cheveyo close behind, with Dan and Ivy trailing. Then— *Snap.* Ivy stepped on a fallen branch. The sound cracked through the silence like a gunshot. The Goblin's head whipped toward them, his yellow eyes glowing like embers. He straightened, his bony frame suddenly rigid. He slinked toward the edge of the cabin, peering around it just as Cash caught sight of him. Two burning eyes. Watching. Cash threw an arm out, stopping the group dead in their tracks. A chilling realization settled over them. They turned. They ran. "To the van!" Cash shouted.

The Van Under Siege

The four of them sprinted through the open field, the van coming into sight just beyond the trees. Cash fumbled in his pocket, his fingers searching for the keys. His heart pounded. Almost there. Then—he dropped them. Cursing under his breath, he skidded to a stop and backtracked. The Goblin was closing in fast. With one final grasp, he snatched up the keys, lunged for the van, and flung himself into the driver's seat. The others banged on the doors, desperate to get inside. But they were locked.

Frantically, Cash reached over and unlocked them. The moment the doors clicked open, they scrambled in. Cash shoved the key into the ignition and pumped the gas. The engine sputtered, coughed—then died. "Come on, come on!" he muttered, turning the key again. Nothing. Cheveyo locked the doors, peering out the window. No sign of the Goblin. But then— Dust. Clouds of dirt swirled around the van, thickening with every passing second. Something was moving, fast, kicking up the earth as it circled them. A blur. A shadow.

Then— A piercing *howl.* "Eeeeeaaaaooooooo!" The sound vibrated through the van, rattling their bones. Ivy clutched Dan, her breath shallow. Cash twisted the key again. The van sputtered—then roared to life. "Hold on!" he shouted. But before he could hit the gas, the van *lurched.* The entire vehicle rocked violently, throwing them in every direction. The engine shuddered—and then died again. Silence. Then, a shadow loomed over the windshield. The Goblin. His scrawny arms trembled under the weight of the van's *battery.*

Cash barely had time to react before the creature let out a shriek and *hurled* the battery straight at the windshield. Glass cracked. The battery bounced off, thudding against the ground. Cash's breath hitched. His gaze flicked upward—past the shattered glass, to the full moon hanging above. A memory flashed through his mind. The well. The Holy Water. The Cahuilla Indian leading him along the trail.

His eyes darted back and forth. A plan was forming. Then—*hissssss.* The van tilted. A tire deflated, sinking one side into the dirt. The vehicle trembled, shifting unevenly beneath them. The Goblin reappeared on Cheveyo's side, pressing his face against the window. His jagged teeth gnashed together, breath fogging the glass. Cheveyo didn't hesitate. He grabbed his flashlight and *blasted* the beam into the Goblin's face. The creature shrieked, retreating into the darkness.

A New Plan

"Guys!" Cash called. "Check the back—I think I still have some fireworks!" Dan and Ivy scrambled over the seats, throwing aside old blankets, gear, and junk. Their hands finally landed on a box buried beneath the clutter. They ripped it open. Inside—fireworks. Big ones. Cash nodded. "We're gonna have to split up." Dan hesitated. "That… didn't go well last time." Cheveyo pulled out a massive red rocket, his grip tightening around it. "We've got this now." Another tire deflated, causing the van to sink even lower. The vehicle tilted, a sharp *groan* emanating from its undercarriage.

No more time. Cash turned to Ivy. "Take Dan and head to the Landlord's RV. Get help. Cheveyo and I will go the other way." Ivy narrowed her eyes. "And what makes you so sure the Goblin is gonna follow *you?*" Cash reached into his pocket, pulling out a handful of jewelry—shiny, golden, stolen from the Goblin's cave. "I was gonna give this back to Lin," he said. "But it doesn't matter anymore." They divided the fireworks. Cheveyo placed his hand on the sliding door handle, glancing at everyone to make sure they were ready.

He took a breath. Then— "On three." A beat. "One… two… three!" The door *slammed* open. They leapt into the night. Dan threw an arm around Ivy, guiding her toward the RV as fast as they could run. Cash and Cheveyo bolted in the opposite direction. The Goblin's yellow eyes glowed beneath the van. In a sudden blur of movement, it scrambled out, its gnarled limbs clawing against the dirt, chasing after Dan and Ivy.

Ivy looked back, and a jolt of terror shot through her. "Aaahhhh! It's coming after us!" Her scream echoed through the night, carrying over to Cash and Cheveyo, who spun around. In the chaos, Dan fumbled with the firecrackers and smoke bombs, sparks flying as he hurled them toward the monstrous creature. Colors of smoke billowed across the ground, swirling in thick plumes, masking their retreat. The Goblin, undeterred, lunged forward.

A skeletal hand shot through the haze, its fingers hooking into Ivy's pant leg. The fabric tore, and a searing pain ripped through her calf. She yelped. Dan grabbed a handful of ground spinners and flung them at the creature. They sparked and whirled in dizzying circles, forcing the Goblin to hop frantically to avoid them. "Ehhee! Yrrriiii! Uuuuah!" it screeched, twisting and writhing in frustration. Cheveyo, watching from a few yards away, knew they needed an edge. He yanked a small rocket from his pack, a crude skull and crossbones painted onto its casing. He struck a match, the fuse igniting in a sharp hiss. "Dodge this!" he growled, letting it fly.

The rocket skittered off the ground before launching toward its target. The Goblin, with unnatural speed, leapt into the air, limbs sprawled wide. The missile shot between its bony legs, missing by inches. "Oooooouuuu!" the Goblin wailed as the rocket continued on, slamming into Barry's RV with a deafening explosion. A charred hole tore through the metal door.

Barry snored peacefully, oblivious to the chaos outside, until the impact of the explosion jolted him upright. "Who's there?!" he shouted, scrambling to his feet. Pounding on the door followed. "Barry, open the door!!" Dan's voice rang through. Ivy's cries were frantic. "The Goblin's after us! Help!" Barry peered through the peephole. Outside, Dan and Ivy were wide-eyed, wild with fear. Through the window, he caught sight of Cash and Cheveyo, their flashlights swinging as they sprinted through the clearing.

His stomach dropped. "Poopsidoo!" Without hesitation, Barry yanked a small key from his pocket and made for the trapdoor in the floor. As he lifted the hatch, he hesitated, glancing toward the kitchen. He darted back, snatched a blue bottle of his prized sake, then scurried down into the hidden storage room, sealing himself away. Cash and Cheveyo scoured the area. The Goblin had vanished, but Cash knew it was still watching. He reached into his pocket and pulled out Lin's gold bracelet. Holding it high, he let the moonlight dance off its polished surface. "Over here, you little toad!" he taunted. "You want this gold? Come and get it!"

From the tangled branches above, the Goblin's slit pupils dilated, catching the golden glow. A forked tongue flicked between jagged teeth. "Eeeee...eeeee...eeee!" It dropped from the tree in a tangle of limbs, its beady gaze locked onto the prize. Cash and Cheveyo took off, leading it deeper into the woods. Cash ran, his breath sharp and ragged. He checked his watch—4:15 AM. Dawn was creeping closer, but not fast enough.

Ahead, the trail split. Cheveyo veered left. Cash skidded to a halt. "Hey, where are you going? The well is this way!" Cheveyo didn't stop. "You go to the well. I'm going to blast his cave!" He held up a large red rocket, determination set in his eyes. "No! Cheveyo, we have to stay together!" "I gotta do this! I'll meet you at the well!" Cash hesitated, then clenched his jaw and pressed forward, leaving Cheveyo to disappear into the darkness.

Holy Water Well

Cash crested the hill, heart hammering. He grabbed a thick branch from the path, brandishing it like a club. Raising the bracelet, he let its glow work its magic. "Come out! I know you want this!" The forest hushed. Even the insects fell silent. Then, from the underbrush, the Goblin slithered forward, eyes fixated on the bracelet. Cash's pulse pounded. "You want this? Come and get it!" The Goblin pulled a dagger from its tattered belt. The blade gleamed under the moonlight. Cash swallowed, trying not to show fear.

Then it lunged. Cash barely dodged in time, swinging his branch wildly. The Goblin darted between the trees, its movements erratic, taking slashes at him. He struck, but the creature was too fast. A flash of movement—a blur of claws—and suddenly the Goblin was on his shoulder. A sharp sting lanced through Cash's arm as the dagger found flesh. He gritted his teeth, grabbed the creature, and flung it to the ground.

The dagger clattered away. Cash lunged for it, fingers grazing the hilt— Too late. The Goblin pounced, wrenching the weapon from his grip. They wrestled, tumbling against the edge of the well. The bracelet dangled precariously between them, catching the moonlight. The Goblin's gaze flickered between the gold and Cash's determined eyes. Then—a distant explosion.

A fiery glow erupted from the direction of the mines. Cheveyo's rocket had found its mark. The Goblin sniffed the air. A guttural cry escaped its throat. "Aaaaiiiiieeeee!" Abandoning Cash, it spun on its heels and bolted into the trees, heading straight for its lair. Cash staggered back, gripping his bleeding arm, watching the creature vanish into the night.

The entrance to the mine was already half-buried in rubble, shaken loose by the first explosion. Cheveyo crouched low, setting the last two rockets just inside the jagged opening. He flicked open his lighter, shielding the flame from the biting wind, but it sputtered and died. Footsteps. Heavy, uneven. Getting closer. Panic surged through him. He flicked the lighter again—nothing. Out of fuel. He cursed, tossing it aside. Desperate, he grabbed two rocks, striking them together. Tiny sparks danced in the darkness. "C'mon!" he hissed. "C'mon!" A shrill screech cut through the night. Then—impact. A hunched, wiry shape slammed into him, clawed hands scrabbling for purchase. Cheveyo staggered under the weight as the Goblin shrieked, sinking its jagged teeth into his ear.

Pain lanced through him. With a roar, he brought the rocks crashing down onto the creature's head. The Goblin wailed and thrashed. They tumbled to the ground in a desperate, frenzied grapple. Dirt and dust choked the air. Cheveyo clawed at the Goblin's cloak, tearing fabric, then snatched up a fistful of earth and flung it into its face. The Goblin reeled back, coughing and rubbing its eyes. Blinded.

Seizing the moment, Cheveyo scrambled for the rockets, his heart hammering. He reached into his pouch, fingers brushing against the fine gold dust. He poured it onto one of the rocks and struck again— A spark. A flicker of light— The Goblin's yellow eyes snapped open, burning with fury. Its pupils, spiderwebbed with blood-red veins, locked onto Cheveyo.

It lunged. The force knocked Cheveyo backward into the mine's gaping maw. A deafening explosion ripped through the night as the rockets ignited. The ground shook. Stones rained down in a relentless cascade on top of Cheveyo. The entrance collapsed. Darkness. A triumphant, maniacal cackle echoed in the night. The Goblin spun away from the rubble, bolting toward the well.

The Trick

Cash paced near the well, scanning the path for any sign of Cheveyo. The wind rattled the trees. His fingers curled into fists. Where was he? Then, movement.

A hunched figure emerged from the shadows, limping, its cloak torn and streaked with blood. The Goblin. It sneered, its sharp teeth bared in a grotesque grin. The wind carried its rasping voice. "My foe… your friend… has come to an end." Cash's grip tightened around the gold bracelet in his hand. "You nasty little Goblin," he spat. "I'm going to make this… disappear."

The Goblin's eyes gleamed with greed as it fixated on the bracelet. Cash moved swiftly, performing a sleight-of-hand trick. The bracelet vanished. The Goblin shrieked. In a frenzy, it lunged, tackling Cash to the ground, clawing at his pockets, raking its nails across his chest. "Gold! Gold! Give it to me!" it screeched. "Where is it?!" Cash writhed beneath its grasp, struggling. "The bucket!" he gasped. "It's in the bucket!"

The Goblin's head snapped up. The bucket hung over the well, swaying gently. The bracelet dangled from the handle. The Goblin leapt onto the edge of the bucket stretching toward the bracelet. Cash rolled onto his side, spotting a loose rock. He grabbed it, sat up, and hurled it at the pulley. He missed. Perched on the bucket's edge, the Goblin cackled with wicked delight. It grinned down at Cash, victorious.

Then— A war cry shattered the night. A silver blade spun through the air, glinting in the moonlight. The ax. It sliced clean through the pulley. The rope unraveled. The bucket dropped. The Goblin yelped as it plunged, disappearing into the depths of the well. A distant splash echoed from below. Cash looked up, panting. Cheveyo stood at the edge of the clearing, disheveled and dust-covered, but alive.

Baptism by Fire

Cash and Cheveyo rushed to the well's edge, peering into the blackness. "The sun's coming up!" Cheveyo gasped. "Aren't we supposed to say something? To finish the baptism?" Cash opened his mouth—but a hand shot up from the well. A filthy, skeletal hand. It latched onto Cheveyo's braid, yanking him downward. Cheveyo fought against the pull, fingers scrabbling for his knife. "Say it! Finish the baptism!" Cash steadied himself, voice ringing through the dawn. "We baptize you in the name of the Father, the Son, and the Holy Spirit!"

Cheveyo slashed the braid. The severed hair slipped through the Goblin's grasp as it tumbled backward, screaming, swallowed by the darkness. A blinding white light burst from the well. The earth trembled. Cracks spread like veins along the stone walls. A golden aura seeped upward, twisting, shimmering. And then—a figure. The Goblin, no longer a twisted creature of greed and malice, but a man. Human once more. His eyes, once yellow with corruption, were clear. He met Cash and Cheveyo's gaze, a flicker of gratitude in his expression. He smiled, bowed his head in acknowledgment, and rose, ascending into the golden haze.

Cash shielded his eyes as the light intensified. The sun crested over the horizon. The haze evaporated. Silence fell. Cash turned to Cheveyo, breathless. "Whoa." Cheveyo exhaled, shaking his head. "No one's going to believe us." Cash followed his gaze to the ax, still lodged above the well. He frowned. "Where did you get that?" Cheveyo glanced back at the mine. "I thought I was trapped. But I found a way out. I thought I was going to die in there."

Cash picked up the severed braid. "That was a close one." The two began their slow trek back toward the cabin. At the bottom of the path, Cash turned for one last look at the well. A piece of the Goblin's torn cloak fluttered in the breeze, caught on the ruined pulley. It was over. The first hints of dawn painted the sky in muted hues as Cash and Cheveyo trudged toward Barry's RV, their clothes torn and bodies exhausted. Cheveyo ran a hand through his now-missing hair, shaking his head. Cash banged on the door.

"Hey, guys, it's us! Open up!" he called. From the cabin's broken doorway, Ivy and Dan rushed toward them. "Cash, Cheveyo! Are you guys okay?" Ivy asked, her face lined with concern. "Yeah, but where's Barry?" Cash asked, glancing at the dark RV. Ivy shook her head. "We knocked all night. He wasn't there." Cheveyo and Cash exchanged uneasy glances. Dan squinted at Cheveyo's unevenly shorn scalp. "What happened to your hair?" Cheveyo sighed. "Long story." "And the Goblin?" Ivy pressed. Cash took a deep breath. "Trapped in the well."

Before anyone could respond, the earth beneath them rumbled. A hidden hatch, camouflaged with dirt and vines, creaked open. Barry emerged, his face weary but relieved. His eyes scanned the group before he exhaled. "The Goblin is gone... for good," he said. "I don't feel him anymore. You did it." A frazzled Lin stumbled from the cabin, her clothes stained with dirt, her eyes sunken with exhaustion. She whined as she saw Cash. "I wanna go home!"

No one responded. Cheveyo crossed his arms. "You hid down there the entire time?" Barry dusted himself off. "Well, yeah! That little devil wasn't getting any help from me." The others stared in disbelief. Barry sighed, running a hand over his face. "I've been cursed for over two hundred years. It could only be broken by someone with a heart of gold. That wasn't me. My heart was ruined by greed." Cash narrowed his eyes. "And now?" Barry smiled faintly. "Now, I owe you a drink. Come inside."

Barry's Gift

They crowded around Barry's dining table, the small space feeling even smaller. Lin sat on the bench, arms crossed, sulking. Barry poured them each a small cup of sake. "A toast!" Barry declared. "I can't tell you how long I've waited to get rid of that little monster. How'd you do it?" "Baptized him," Cash said simply. "In the holy water well." Barry froze. "Where?" "Near the old mines." A strange look crossed Barry's face. "That well… That's where I used to meet my darling Sara." Silence settled over the table. "How did you know?" Barry asked. "Someone shared a story with me on our hike yesterday." Barry chuckled bitterly. "I wish I'd known that a long time ago."

He turned, pulled out an old key ring, and carefully selected a single silver key. He held it between his fingers before pressing it into Cash's palm. "What's this?" Cash asked, staring at the engraved horse on the key's surface. "A gift. This will take you home."

Everyone exchanged puzzled glances. "Go down the road past the windmill," Barry continued. "You'll see an old red barn to the right. It's in there." As the group moved to leave, Lin lingered near a shelf. A beautiful crystal bottle caught her eye. She hesitated—then slipped it into her pocket. Barry saw but said nothing. "One more thing," he called as they stepped outside. They turned. "Don't ever come back. These woods are full of curses." The RV door shut. A heavy sigh escaped Barry's lips as he leaned against it. "One curse down," he muttered, finishing his drink. "A dozen more to go."

As they walked, Lin lagged behind, dragging her suitcase. "What did he mean, more curses?" Dan mused. "I don't wanna know," Ivy said. "I just wanna get outta here." "Yeah. Me too," Cash muttered. The large wooden doors groaned as Cheveyo and Dan pulled them apart. Dust swirled in the golden light filtering through the cracks. A covered shape loomed in the center. Cash grabbed the cloth and yanked it free. A stunning 1968 green Mustang Fastback gleamed in the sunlight.

Everyone gasped. "Whoa!" Cheveyo breathed. "She's a beauty." Dan ran a finger along the chrome. "Nice ride." "Ooooo, Cash! From now on, you drive everywhere!" Ivy grinned. Lin approached cautiously. She caught her reflection in the window and shrieked. "Oh my gosh! My hair! And my face!" Cheveyo popped the trunk. They loaded their belongings inside—except Lin's oversized suitcase. "This won't fit," Cash said. "You'll have to keep it on your lap." Lin scowled as Dan pulled up the seat for her and Ivy. He dumped the suitcase onto Lin's lap before climbing into the front passenger seat. Cash slid behind the wheel.

Cheveyo leaned into the window. "Let's see if she starts." Cash turned the ignition. The engine roared to life. Cheveyo whooped. "Drive safe!" Cash revved the engine, then peeled out of the barn, leaving a cloud of dust behind. Cheveyo coughed, laughing as he brushed the dust from his jacket. He shook his head as the Mustang disappeared down the road.

Rain began to fall. It was dark and stormy when Cash and his friends found themselves winding through the mist-covered mountain roads. The headlights of their old Mustang sliced through the fog, casting long shadows along the uneven path. Up ahead, the towering figure of the Grizzly Bear sculpture loomed in the distance, a silent warden guarding the entrance to Big Bear. As the car roared past, a gust of wind swept through, sending a swirl of dead leaves into the air, spinning them like ghosts in the night. The car was silent, the soft rain tapping on the windows. They reached the gate to Lin's large estate, which stood shut. Lin stuck her hand out the window and called, 'It's me—open up!' The gate creaked open, and they drove in. The green Mustang rolled up the driveway and came to a stop. 'Glad we made it back in one piece,' Dan said, grinning as he stretched his legs, finally free from the cramped car. Ivy, looking somewhat relieved, muttered, "Let's not go back to Big Bear anytime soon." Cash gave a wry smile. "We won't."

He slammed the trunk shut with a decisive thud, and his friends climbed into their car, driving away into the night. Cash lingered for a moment, staring at the spot where they had just been. Then, with a slow sigh, he returned to the Mustang, started the engine, and turned the car around. Lin appeared at the front of her house, leaning against the wrought iron gate as it opened. "Where are you going, Cash?" Lin's voice was soft but carried a weight that seemed to hang in the air between them.

Cash's face fell, a mix of frustration and guilt welling up within him. "I'll be back tomorrow to pick up my things," he said, avoiding her gaze. Lin's pride was unyielding, she only nodded. "Make sure to leave the key when you're done." She turned away, gathering her belongings as she headed towards the green door. Without another word, Cash pulled out of the driveway, his eyes fixed on the road ahead, not daring to glance back. The car rolled away into the night, its headlights cutting through the fog that seemed to press in from all sides.

Silent Reflections

The Mustang rumbled through the hills, its engine a low hum beneath the quiet hum of the night. Cash's mind wandered as he drove, his fingers resting lightly on the wheel. The wind rushed through the open windows, cooling his heated thoughts. Above, a flock of birds soared across the sky, their wings stretching as if they, too, were trying to escape the weight of the world.

He didn't know where he was going, but for the first time in weeks, he felt the weight on his shoulders lift. As he pulled into the Observatory, the moon low in the sky, casting pale blue hues over the city. The parking lot was filled with families lounging on the grass, their laughter ringing through the air like a melody. Couples strolled hand in hand, oblivious to the world around them. Cash walked past them, the evening air cool against his skin, and made his way up to the viewing area.

He leaned against the railing, gazing out at the sprawling city below, its lights twinkling like stars on the horizon. The music of a nearby trio of classical musicians drifted towards him. A group of children nearby began to twirl and dance in time to the melodies, their joy infectious. Cash smiled, a brief flicker of warmth in his heart. For a moment, everything felt right. The weight of the world, the tangled mess of his life, seemed to fade away. Here, in this place, he could just be—alive, breathing, existing.

Back at Lin's house, night had fallen. Lin stood in front of her vanity, the soft glow of the dim lamp casting shadows across the room. She wore a pink robe, slippers matching the color, her hair wrapped in a towel. The beauty mask on her face gleamed under the light as she admired the crystal bottle that had come into her possession, a relic of something much darker. She walked to the vase by the window, plucking a single flower and placing it carefully inside the bottle. The vase was old, its surface cracked and faded, but it had served its purpose. Lin paused before the framed photo of her and Cash, a picture from a time when everything had been different. Her fingers brushed the glass before she set the photo aside, face down, as if trying to bury the past.

With a sigh, she removed the mask and continued her nightly ritual, the steady rhythm of her actions grounding her. She applied moisturizer to her face, her movements slow and methodical. When she turned off the light and climbed into bed, the room was still. The moonlight filtered through the window, casting a silvery glow across the room. The crystal bottle, now placed upon the vanity, began to shimmer, its surface crackling as if alive. Golden particles burst from it, swirling in the air before they disappeared completely. The flower within the bottle fell to its side, lifeless.

The night was quiet, broken only by the soft chirping of crickets and the distant call of an owl. Barry's RV trailer sat against the indigo sky, its silhouette dark and foreboding. The air was cool, and the sound of movement from within broke the silence.

Inside, the orange glow of a lamp flickered as Barry poured himself a drink, his mind elsewhere. He sat at the table, his fingers absently tracing the edges of an old photograph. It was a picture from the early 1900s, of men standing on the docks of a sea port. One of the men, wearing a cap, held the very crystal bottle Lin had taken from Barry. The same cap that now rested on Barry's own head.

As he gazed at the photo, Barry's eyes drifted to the empty shelf where the bottle had once been. A faint shimmer filled the air, and in the blink of an eye, the bottle reappeared, glowing with an ethereal golden light. Barry chuckled to himself, taking a long sip from his glass. "Well, well," he muttered. "It's good to have you back."

The Gift of the Goblin

Cash pulled into a small motel parking lot, the headlights of the Mustang illuminating the cracked asphalt beneath. He parked the car, his movements slow and deliberate as he reached into the trunk for his jacket and backpack. But as he lifted his jacket, something fell out and caught his eye—something sparkling in the dim light.

He bent down and picked it up, holding it under the streetlight. A ruby-colored gemstone gleamed in his palm, its surface smooth and warm to the touch. "What the heck... Where'd you come from?" Cash whispered, his voice tinged with disbelief. A chill wind swept past him, and in that moment, he heard a faint, mocking laugh—the sound of something ancient and mischievous. Cash froze, his eyes darting around. A shadow flickered at the edge of his vision, twisting and turning like a living thing. His heart skipped a beat. Then, as though mocking his fears, the shadow shifted into the shape of a small boy in a red hoodie. The child laughed and danced before running to his mother's side. Cash exhaled sharply, shaking his head. He closed the trunk and turned away, but the unease still lingered in his chest.

A New Beginning

Months passed, and life got better. Cash sat in a quiet coffee shop, a steaming cup of tea in front of him, and Dan across from him, his eyes alight with excitement. "I'm going to propose to Ivy next month," Dan said, pulling out a small velvet box from his pocket. Inside, a delicate ring sparkled, its beauty catching the sunlight. Cash smiled, his heart genuinely happy for his friend. "You two make a great couple." Dan's face softened. "I want you to be my best man." Cash's smile widened. "Of course, but on one condition." Dan raised an eyebrow. "What's that?" "No bachelor's party in Big Bear," Cash said with a chuckle. Dan laughed, agreeing immediately. "Deal," Cash said, shaking Dan's hand.

Dan leaned back in his chair, grinning. "So, how's the music going?" "Good!" Cash replied with a smile. "I just released a new album called *Mindful*. It's got twelve tracks. I recorded it all in about a month. Really fun and easy." "Nice!" Dan said, impressed. "No record deal or anything?" "Nah, I just put it out myself—streaming, social media, all that. It came out great. I'm happy with it." Dan nodded, looking thoughtful. "That's awesome.

You only need one song to go viral, and boom—you've got a career for life." Cash raised an eyebrow. "Really? You think so?" "Absolutely!" Dan said with a grin. "I believe in you, man. It just takes a little time." Dan glanced at his watch. "Hey, I've gotta run. I'm cooking dinner tonight. You're welcome to join us if you want—might be some single ladies there. Ivy's having friends over."

Dan stood, gave Cash a wink, and slapped him on the shoulder. "Catch you later, man."

Cash leaned back in his chair, a thought crossing his mind. Maybe it was time to stop trying to solve everything—and just let the pieces fall where they may. As he turned his Rubik's Cube in his hands, the final move clicked into place. All the colors aligned. For the first time in a long while, Cash felt like his own life had just done the same. Just as he was about to get up to leave, a voice broke through his thoughts. "Moon, Medium Green Tea Latte?" Cash looked up and spotted a brunette ahead of him in line. Her floral dress caught his attention. When she turned, their eyes met, and for a fleeting moment, everything else faded away. "Moon?" Cash asked, surprised. "Cash?" Moon's voice carried the same disbelief. Drawn together as if by fate, they closed the space between them with a warm embrace. The joy in their eyes filled the room with sunshine. Somewhere in the background, Cash's new song played on the radio, its melody warm and full of life. The pieces had finally fallen into place. Moon pulled back, a playful smile tugging at her lips. "So, you still getting into trouble, or did you finally settle down?" Cash chuckled, shaking his head. "You wouldn't believe the things I've seen." Moon laughed softly. "Somehow, I think I would. Tell me all about it." Cash smiled, the weight of the past finally lifting from his shoulders.

The End.

About the Author

Hello – My name is Eric David Wallace, and I'm a music artist and film director from Los Angeles. After spending ten years trying to break into Hollywood without success, I moved to Seattle to pursue my music career.

I wrote *Goblin* during the pandemic in 2020, hoping to turn it into a film. When I couldn't secure a producer, studio, or investor, I decided to adapt the screenplay into a novel and try my luck in the book world. My goal is to use the profits from this book to finance the movie—so if you've made it this far, thank you. You're helping bring *Goblin* one step closer to the big screen.

Writing this story has been both a creative journey and a deeply personal one. I hope you enjoyed reading *Goblin* as much as I enjoyed writing it. And remember—*all that glitters is not gold.*

If you're curious about my work, check out my first feature film, *Love Dream*, a zero-budget project now available on Amazon. I've written more screenplays, so if this goes well, I'll do it again!

Thanks for spending time with me.

Goblin Official Website: **goblinfilm.com**
Watch my Films: **arc26.com**
Listen to my Music: **ericdavidwallace.com**

To everyone who has supported me on this journey—thank you, both people and goblins alike. And to the producers who passed on this... you'll wish you hadn't, for your regrets will soon be granted.